MYSTERY
bmc

LET DEAD ENOUGH ALONE

W9-BUD-904

LET DEAD ENOUGH ALONE

A Captain Heimrich Mystery

Richard and Frances Lockridge

Chivers Press • G.K. Hall & Co.
Bath, Avon, England • Thorndike, Maine USA

This Large Print edition is published by Chivers Press, England, and by G. K. Hall & Co., USA.

Published in 1995 in the U.K. by arrangement with the authors' estate.

Published in 1995 in the U.S. by arrangement with HarperCollins Publishers, Inc.

U.K. Hardcover ISBN 0–7451–2994–3 (Chivers Large Print)
U.S. Softcover   ISBN 0–7838–1159–4 (Nightingale Collection Edition)

The text of this Large Print edition is unabridged.
Other aspects of the book may vary from the original edition.

Set in 16 pt. New Times Roman.

Printed in Great Britain on acid-free paper.

British Library Cataloguing in Publication Data available

Library of Congress Cataloging-in-Publication Data

Lockridge, Richard, 1898–
    Let dead enough alone : a Captain Heimrich mystery / Richard and Frances Lockridge.
        p. cm.
    ISBN 0–7838–1159–4 (lg. print : sc)
    1. Large type books.
    2. Heimrich, M. L. (Fictitious character—Fiction.
    3. Police—New York (State)—Fiction.
    I. Lockridge, Frances Louise Davis.   II. Title.
[PS3523.O245L47   1995]
813'.52—dc20   94–33676

CHAPTER ONE

Asked why, Margaret Halley said because it would be good for both of them. She said this with decision, as she said most things. She said they needed a change of scene; to do something which they did not always do or, indeed, had ever done.

'I have,' her husband said. 'When I was younger, to be sure. Which is rather to the point.'

He was told that he spoke as if he were an old man.

'Which,' Margaret said, 'is not good for you, John. Not in the least good for you.'

'And going to the country in mid-winter, having a party—a New Year's Eve party—there, would be good for me? It would—what, my dear?'

'Stimulate,' Margaret said. 'Part of therapy is to—'

'Again,' John said. 'There is nothing the matter with me, my dear. With all respect, of course. Speaking as a layman.'

She made a quick gesture of rejection, as of a remark not worth listening to. She said that, of course, there was nothing the matter with him. As, she added, she told him perhaps too often, since, if one wanted complete accuracy, that was a statement which could be made to, and

1

of, no one.

'In the simplest terms,' Margaret said, 'I should like to get away for a few days. You have imagination. You should realize that a steady diet of—' She did not finish, except by a movement of her hands. She had very attractive hands, John Halley thought. Still. She would not like the 'still' and, in fact, its use—even its use in the quiet of his mind—was almost as unjust as it was ungenerous. She was, to be sure, a few years over forty. She was, in her fashion, quite beautiful. It was not necessary at all to say that she was 'still' quite beautiful. In another fifteen years, perhaps. If she lived so long.

'It's what you want,' he said. 'There would be no reason otherwise. As we both know.'

'Of course,' she said. 'As we both know. But not every day, day in day out. I see enough of what that does. Helps to do.' She smiled at him. They sat on either side of a bright fire—a fire which seemed all the brighter because it did not need to warm; a small fire, nurtured for its gayety. Her smile was as quick as one of the little, jumping flames. 'There won't be any strain in it,' she said. 'We can get the Speeds. Have them there a day or two before. They'll see to everything.'

'Strain?' he said. 'I hadn't thought of it as a strain. Why do you call it strain?'

'A chore, then,' she said. 'It won't be even that. And—it will be as good for you as for me.'

2

She paused to light a cigarette. She was unhurried—fitted the cigarette carefully into a long holder, flicked flame from a table lighter, inhaled deeply. That done, she held the cigarette package up for an instant, and toward John Halley. He shook his head.

'It's a mistake to settle so completely into the familiar,' she said. 'To accept the familiar as the inevitable. It can become a retreat—one of the retreats. A surface peace, but actually a kind of sloth. Underneath, in the subconscious, there can be a building up—' She broke off. She used her cigarette in its long holder as a kind of pointer at her husband. 'We're not old,' she said. 'Not by any means. It's not healthy to think we're old.'

'I haven't thought that,' he said. 'Or—that we—I, at any rate—are precisely young. After fifty—'

His face was thin, and rather long. His hair had receded, so that now the heightened forehead added to the length of his face. There was a slight depression—hardly more than a flattening—of the bones at the top of the skull, and now this lay just, but only just, beyond the hairline. (The knowledge of this, then fully hidden, imperfection had worried John Halley when he had been much younger.) The skin of his face and forehead, and of his long, thin hands, was deeply browned.

'In the simplest words,' she said. 'In the layman's words. You brood. That's the reason, as much as anything.'

'For this party?'

'Specifically. For what it represents.'

'What it represents,' he said, 'is a drive of sixty miles or so. A house that hasn't been lived in for months. The starting up of the furnace. The turning on of water. The—'

'That's it,' she said. 'What I was getting at, John. The piling up of obstacles. Until they block the way. I told you, the Speeds will do all that. Go up several days ahead. Get in all we need. If the lake's frozen, we'll skate. Build a big bonfire and—'

'I gather you've already arranged it? Written the Speeds or telephoned them?'

She smiled, this time slowly.

'So that now it is really easier to go than not?'

Still smiling, she nodded her head. She had, had always had, the—the *neatest* head. The hair was like a black cap, the conformation of the skull under the hair delicately precise. A precision instrument, all of Margaret Halley, her husband thought. He said, 'The lake almost never freezes before mid-January. Not for skating. At least, it almost never did, as I remember.'

'Don't go back into it,' she said. 'It's bad for you, all this going back into the past.'

'You take your patients there,' he said. 'That's the—therapy, isn't it?'

'Under direction,' she said. 'For a purpose.

4

Under control, to find a cause, not a hiding place. But you know that. About the party?'

'It seems to be settled, doesn't it?' Halley said. He looked at his wife curiously, as if seeking to read in her face some thing beyond her words. He smiled faintly. 'Why do you so often treat me as one of your patients, Margaret?' he said. He spoke with no insistence, as if the matter were of little concern.

She looked at him steadily through eyes which were almost black.

'Well,' he said, 'how am I, doctor?'

'You'll be all right,' she said.

'But aren't now?'

'You're fine,' she said. 'We'll go up the day before, then? Thursday, that will be. Stay over Monday?'

'However you've planned it,' he said.

'Invite—whoever we invite—for Friday afternoon. So that, if they like, they can get there before dark. The three forty two, for those who come by train. Speed can meet them in the wagon.'

'However you say. But—it may be a little difficult to catch your guests, mayn't it? They may lack enthusiasm. As I did.'

She shook her head. She said she did not think so.

'Probably you're right,' he said. 'Tom Kemper, I suppose? But naturally, Kemper.'

'And Miss Latham,' Margaret said. 'Dear

5

Audrey.'

'We're both very understanding,' he said, with no particular inflection. 'Both so civilized. So—what would you say, doctor? So well adjusted?'

'Did you want it any other way? Ever?'

He reached to a table near his chair and took a cigar from a humidor. He clipped the end of the cigar with the blade of a little silver knife, and held his hand toward Margaret, who put the table lighter in it. He thanked her before he held the cigar's end in the little flame, leaning forward as he did so. As he started the cigar the flame lessened and grew bright, lessened and grew bright so that, in the softly lighted room, light wavered on his brown face.

He had not answered.

'You look tired,' she said. 'Depressed.'

'How could I be?' he said. 'I do nothing. And, I have what I want. Have always had. As you mention so often. Kemper and Audrey, then. And—who else, my dear?'

CHAPTER TWO

The important thing was that she had been able to decide. That, she realized now, was always the important thing. Only those who had been through it could understand; only those who had been in that dim, gray place where choice

6

was impossible. Even now, with all of it over and not to recur—Margaret Halley said it would not recur—she remembered with that familiar twinge of terror, that sudden coldness in the mind. She sat again at a restaurant table, with the menu in her hands—trembling a little as her hands trembled. And she could not decide between creamed chicken and broiled spring lamb chop (one).

If you tried to explain, explanation was ridiculous. But that was as clear to you as to anyone. The choice was trivial; it did not matter to yourself or to the waitress or to anyone whether you said, 'The creamed chicken, please,' or 'The lamb chop, I think.' But you sat there, the menu trembling in your hands, and your mind was numb, and full of fear. (Finally, she had sat shaking her head slowly from side to side, and then she had begun to cry at the dreariness of the world, and in pity for herself, and had got up, still crying slowly, and gone out into the darkness of a sun-flooded street. It was after that that her father had taken her to Margaret.)

'The dark year,' she called it, in her mind, and it had been only a year, or a little more than a year. (A short piece of iron piping, probably fallen from a truck, was on the pavement in front of her. She could swerve the car to one side. She could straddle the pipe. Without thinking of it, she steered so as to straddle, and only after some seconds realized

7

that she had done so, making this decision without thought, as such decisions must be made—without thought, without hesitation. Two years ago she could not any longer drive a car—or choose between black shoes and brown.)

Asked by Dr Margaret Halley whether she would like to drive into the country, to spend the New Year's weekend in the big Halley house by the lake, she had chosen instantly, and chosen to accept. It was another proof of her complete recovery, another assurance that she was through the dark year, as Margaret had promised her she would be. It had only been necessary—but how difficult!—to understand that such things happened to minds, not only to hers but to many, and that this understanding, and time, would bring her back, and bring the sun back.

She was Lynn Ross again—all of Lynn Ross. The little things which had worried her so much, the little failures, were no longer important. They remained parts of Lynn Ross, but she herself was whole. She was a tall—oh, *too* tall still—woman of twenty-four, driving northeast beyond Bedford Hills, where the parkway ended, following careful directions toward Lake Carabec. She would reach Katonah soon, and must turn north, to a fork three miles beyond, then right for another two miles to a fork. At the fork the road to the left led to the club, which was closed in winter; the

8

road to the right, which she must take, circled the lake. Half way around the lake, opposite the clubhouse—which could be seen now that the leaves were gone—was the Halley house. The house was to the right, the boathouse to the left.

It was three-thirty on the afternoon of Friday, December thirty-first. She would, easily, arrive before dark, although already the light was dimming. She flicked on the car radio and, after it had warmed, pressed the foot button which selected stations. The indicator stopped. '—are feared lost,' the radio said. 'Here is the weather: Increasing northeast winds this afternoon and tonight, with a chance of some snow. Lowest temperature tonight in the upper twenties in the city and along the coast, and in the low twenties in the normally colder interior. Tomorrow partly cloudy and continued moderately cold. This is WNEW, the radio station of the *Daily News*, New York's picture newspaper.'

Well, you had to expect winter when it was winter. And in the country, particularly, some snow was appropriate. The newspapers that morning had, to be sure, said nothing of snow, in any quantity, but had promised fair skies and temperatures rising into the low forties. Apparently something had—

It was evident that something had. Fine snow began to drive against the windshield, melting on the warmth of the glass. Lynn Ross

9

switched the wipers on. She was glad it had held off as long as it had.

The snow was not white, but a gray darkness. Lynn switched on her headlights. The light beams hit a curtain of snow and from it, bounced back into her eyes. She dipped the lights, and that was better. But now snow rushed at the windshield and, just before it reached the glass, swirled upward, dizzy with its own movement—and dizzying to her. Then there were street lights as she went into Katonah, driving now very slowly. The lights made a difference. She went past the station and, beyond it, turned left. After a block, she turned right onto Route 35. That was what Margaret had told her to do.

The snow which had fallen blew toward her on the pavement, netting the black surface with tracings of white. There was still not enough to cause uneasiness, but soon there would be. She wished she had started half an hour earlier from the city; wished she had driven faster while she could. She watched her speedometer; the numerals which gauged the distance she had driven moved up into place with exasperating slowness.

But finally she had driven the three miles, and the tires still had pavement to cling to. Beyond was a bridge. 'Just before you cross the bridge.' She turned right, onto a road which climbed in a steep curve—a narrower road, but still black paved. Two miles now to a fork. The

10

road climbed in an S-curve and here, for the first time, the car skidded slightly. She caught it, and the motor labored. She shifted down, very carefully, fearing the wheels would spin. They did not, and she ground slowly on. It was much darker, now, and even the lowered beams of light reflected into her eyes from what seemed a wall of snow. There was a center line of white, and she guided on that. A mile and one tenth—and two tenths—and three tenths. A mile and a half—a mile and six—a mile and—

She came to the top of the hill, as the speedometer '9' climbed reluctantly in the column of tenths. Here the fork should be. There was no fork—yes, there was a fork. Here the road divided to circle Lake Carabec. She followed the branch to the right. For the first time, here, the snow lay smoothly on the road. But it was so light, still, that her wheels bit through it. In the mirror, she could see the tracks the car left as it ground slowly on the narrow, winding road.

She came around a rock-outcropping, to which a single tree clung perilously, black against the snowy night. Then she was looking over the lake—a black lake which seemed to stretch endlessly into the falling snow. (But it was, Margaret had told her, only a small lake.) The road ran close to it; the guard rail between road and steeply pitching bank looked ancient—a guide, rather than a barrier.

Skidding into it, a car—

Well, the point was not to skid into it. She drove carefully, thankful that the lake lay to the left. She hugged the right side of the road. She skidded again, gently, and caught the skid, but then skidded—just perceptibly—the other way.

She had come a mile since the fork. Another mile—Then, some distance ahead, she saw a lighted house. It was a big house, and there seemed to be lights in all its windows. 'If it's dark, we'll light the place like a Christmas tree,' Margaret had promised. The road pitched down, and she let the motor brake. It levelled and she had not skidded. A mile and six—and seven—and—

Something sparkled ahead and to the right, in the car lights. And eight tenths—and nine— The sparkling was from a reflecting sign. It read, 'John Halley.' She turned into the driveway it marked, and now climbed again and turned again—and skidded. But now the skidding meant nothing, and she drove confidently toward the gayly lighted house. A porch light came on, and a man came around the house, from the rear, with a flashlight. He motioned, beckoned with the flashlight, and pointed with it to the right. She went as directed; a garage, open, was ahead. She drove into the garage, neatly between a station wagon—headed out—and a big sedan. She cut the motor and then the lights. She said,

12

'Whew,' softly, drawing the sound in through pursed lips. The man with the light came to the side of the car.

'Bad night, miss,' he said. 'Bad and gettin' worse. You got bags, miss?'

She had. She got out. She unlocked the trunk and looked down at the small, round, man who pulled her suitcase—'Dinner dress. Slacks and sweater. Nothing in between.' That was what Margaret had advised—and an overnight bag from the trunk of the little car.

'Name's Abner Speed,' the small man said. 'You'd be Miss Ross?'

'Yes,' the tall girl said. She was so *much* taller than this small man.

'Take 'em in for you,' Abner Speed said. 'Just gettin' ready to go for the others.' He indicated the station wagon with a nod of his head. 'Been putting on chains,' he said. 'You got chains with you?'

'No,' she said.

'Anyway, you're here,' Abner told her. 'Hour or so road'll be bad without chains.' He started out of the garage. 'Or with them,' he added. 'Quickest just to cut across here, miss.'

He cut across there, on a snowy path, toward the porch. The door opened, and Margaret Halley stood in it and called, 'Lynn?'

'Yes,' Lynn said, and remembered, and walked tall—walked as tall as she could walk.

('When you learn to do that,' Margaret had said, 'you'll have learned a lot. The highest

13

heels. The straightest back. You're—what, Miss Ross?'

'Five ten.'

'You carry your head forward. Did you know that? You slump your shoulders. You—yes, you wear low heels.'

'I know. I've always been—gawky. "My big gawky girl. My giantess," Dad used to—'

She had been lying down; Margaret had been sitting behind her, in shadows.

'You're beginning to understand,' Margaret had said. 'Part of it. Part of what causes your depression—what we call a simple depression. Remember, when you get up, you're six feet tall. You're taller. You hold your head up and your shoulders up. And—you get shoes with the highest heels you can walk on.'

'I don't understand, doctor. I've always—')

Now she walked along a path, through the snow, in the highest heels she could walk on. (Which, just now, was of course a little silly.) She tried to be as tall—as tall as a tree. Margaret came to the edge of the porch and held out both hands to her. 'I'm so glad you could come,' Margaret Halley said.

'So am I, doctor,' Lynn said. She looked down at Margaret, who looked up at her, who smiled and waited. 'Margaret,' Lynn said.

'Better,' Margaret said. 'Abner—wait a second, Abner.' Abner Speed had started to walk back toward the garage. 'Stop at Ringstead's, will you?' Margaret said. 'Get this

14

filled.'

'Don't know as I'll have time,' Abner said. 'Have to go slow, m'am.'

'If you have time, then,' Margaret said. 'I'm sure you will, Abner.'

Speed said, 'Yes, Mrs Halley,' although without conviction. He went on toward the garage.

Lynn followed Margaret Halley into the brightness of the house—into a square entrance hall, from it into a long living room. A fire burned brightly there, in a big fireplace. Lynn was told she must be frozen; that she must have a drink. Or tea? She decided on tea; was told to back up to the fire, get warm from the fire; that tea wouldn't take a minute. If it was trouble—?

It was none, Margaret—this Margaret so different from Dr Margaret Halley, in her Park Avenue office—told Lynn Ross. It was not, of course, a matter merely of ringing. There were only Lucinda and Abner, and Lucinda would be deep in things. 'Roughing it,' Margaret said, walking toward the end of the big room. 'Aren't you glad it snowed? So appropriate.'

It was that, Lynn thought, warm by the fire, standing with her back to the fire. She looked across at windows—windows almost, but not quite, curtained. In the light which escaped into the night, snowflakes danced. It was most appropriate; it was very pretty. It was pleasant to watch it, from inside, with back to fire.

15

Margaret was not long. She came back with a silver teapot, and silver cream pitcher and sugar bowl, and cups, on a tray. She put the tray down on a table. She said, 'Now,' in a tone of anticipation. 'I'm so glad you got here before the others.' She poured tea. 'John's resting,' she said. 'I insisted he rest. The poor—' She did not finish. Instead, she said she hoped Lynn had had no trouble finding them.

'None,' Lynn said. 'The directions were perfect—Margaret.' She hesitated a moment before the name. It was still more natural to say 'Doctor.' It was still natural to be a little—well, not in awe, precisely. Respectful, austere as the word was, was still perhaps nearer it. But it was easier here. What a pretty woman she is, Lynn thought. And she must be—oh, over forty.

'Isn't Mr Halley well?' she asked.

'John? Oh—well enough. There have been things to do, of course. And it's been months since either of us has turned a muscle. You know how it is.'

Lynn did not, particularly. There was no point in going into it. She sipped tea and the warmth caressed her—caressed slender body, long, slim legs. She opened the jacket of her suit, to feel the warmth through the thinner material of her blouse. She said she felt like purring.

'By all means,' Margaret said. They sipped, for a moment, in silence. 'You'll like the others, I think,' Margaret said, then. 'Shall I brief you

16

about them?'

It always helped to be briefed. Lynn said it always helped.

'Brian Perry,' Margaret said. 'You've heard of him?'

'Should I have?' Lynn asked, shaking her head as she spoke. (I do feel like purring, she thought.) 'Is he somebody famous?'

'I suppose not,' Margaret Halley said. 'Not to everybody. *Doctor* Brian Perry?'

'No,' Lynn said. 'I'm very ignorant. But you know that.'

Margaret looked at her sharply, for an instant with doctor's eyes. Lynn was watching the fire.

'He's a psychiatrist, too,' Margaret said. 'And a neurologist. He's done some very interesting things. Got suggestive results. Has some interesting theories. Of course, some of the theories—' She did not finish that. 'A tall man, Lynn. Much taller than you. Tall and thin—his women patients probably fall in love with him. Which can be helpful, you know. Up to a point. He used to come to the lake summer weekends. They had a little place near the club.'

'The tall dark one will be Dr Perry,' Lynn said. 'You said "they"?'

'He and his wife,' Margaret said. 'She's dead. She was named Carla.'

It would be too bad not to be alive, Lynn thought—Lynn who, not much over a year

17

ago, had taken one sleeping pill and then another, and after that another and another still, because the world was dreary and life stuck in her throat. She said, 'That's too bad,' of Carla Perry, whom she had never known and who was dead. The words were as good as any.

'And Struthers Boyd,' Margaret said. 'They have a house down the road. He and John play golf together. It's too bad Grace is in Florida. You'd like Grace, I think.'

Grace presumably was Boyd's wife. She was not dead. She was in Florida.

'Big man,' Margaret said. 'Very hearty. The—the classmate type. And a man named Kemper—Tom Kemper. And Audrey Latham. Did you ever hear of Audrey Latham?'

She had, it appeared to Lynn, heard of no one. She shook her head, and listened. She heard that Audrey Latham wrote music. 'Show songs. Usually about somebody who can't forget somebody. You know?'

'Yes,' Lynn said.

'Additional music by Audrey Latham, so far,' Margaret said. 'John thinks she's very good, however. Or will be. John's always been interested in music, you know.'

It was another thing that Lynn had not known. But she knew very little of John Halley—that he was older than his wife, and had a great deal of money, and had always had.

18

'In music,' Margaret said. 'In pictures. In writing. He wrote a little himself as a young man, you know.' Once more Lynn had to shake her head. 'When he lived in France,' Margaret said. 'Little sketches. About things—people—little incidents. Charming little things. It was a long time before John and I met—heavens, I must have been in rompers. If in anything. More tea?'

Lynn took more tea.

'And that's all,' Margaret said. 'Brian and Struthers Boyd and Tom and Miss Latham—and John and I, and you. Not a large party—and one too many men, because Grace had her reservations all made for Florida. But—'

She paused. She put her teacup down and lighted a cigarette.

'To be quite honest,' she said, 'John's been moody lately. Hasn't had much interest in things. There's a little therapy in the party, my dear. Pretty young women—you and Miss Latham. John's quite interested in pretty young women, too. Mental stimulation—Brian. *Gemütlichkeit*—good old Struthers. And auld lang syne and whatnot. A bright start for the New Year. And—'

She paused again. She ground out the cigarette she had just lighted and finished the tea in her cup.

'Forget about the therapy,' she said. 'We'll all have fun. More tea?'

'No,' Lynn said.

'It's a dull thing, tea,' Margaret said. 'We'll have cocktails when the others get here or—now, if you like?'

'When the others come. I wonder if—'

'Of course,' Margaret said. 'You want to freshen up. Come, I'll show you.'

She got up; she led Lynn to the hall again and then, insisting on carrying the suitcase while Lynn carried the smaller bag, up the stairs and down a hall to a room at the rear of the house. It was a small room, but on a corner, with two windows. A bath opened off it.

'A lovely room,' Lynn said, and to that Margaret smiled only. She said that she hoped Lynn wouldn't mind an electric blanket.

'Mind?' Lynn said. 'Why?'

'Some people are afraid they'll catch on fire,' Margaret said. 'Some people are afraid of so many things.'

'I'm not,' Lynn said. 'Not any more. I don't remember I ever was of electric blankets.'

'No,' Margaret said. 'Of course not. We'll have a drink or two before we change. And then change. And then have a drink or two.' She went to the door. She stopped there. 'You're fine now, aren't you, my dear?' she said.

'Fine,' Lynn said. 'Just fine, doctor.'

'Time,' Margaret said. 'That almost always does it. Time—and being watched over. I was never in doubt about you, you know. Not about you. In half an hour or so?'

20

Lynn nodded, and Margaret went out of the room and down the hall. Lynn could hear her heels clicking on the uncarpeted floor. Lynn opened her suitcase and took out a dinner dress—a long dress, which was made to fit closely—to make her tall—and hung it in the closet. She 'freshened up.' After a time she heard, from downstairs, the sound of voices, and of a woman's laughter. The laughter sounded gay.

Lynn Ross went down the stairs—a tall girl and very slim, with a wide white forehead and dark eyes, with reddish-brown hair which had a kind of glow in its color, a glow independent of the light which fell on it. She met the others—Dr Brian Perry, who was, as promised, taller than she; who was somewhere in his early forties (probably) and on whose rather long face rimless glasses suggested austerity; Mr Boyd, a loosely large man and a hearty one; a pretty young woman who came to Lynn's shoulder, was very blond, and looked rather more likely to sing songs than to write them. And Tom Kemper, who had— Lynn realized only after she saw him—not been described at all. He was her height or a little less (still she noticed height before almost anything), wore brown hair in a crew cut, and looked at the world with, it seemed, abounding amiability. 'Warm brown eyes.' Lynn had read about them. Here they were, in the open countenance of Mr Kemper, who looked to be

21

in his early thirties, and without a care in the world—who somehow, without saying anything so obvious, managed to say that, for years, he had been waiting for just this delightful opportunity of meeting a tall young woman named Lynn Ross.

Abner Speed—wearing a white coat, now—wheeled in a bar wagon and stood beside it and looked at Dr Margaret Halley. Then, it appeared, there was a momentary hitch. 'I think Mr Halley would rather—' Margaret said, and looked, quickly, toward the door which led to the central hall and the stairs which rose from it. 'I wonder what's—' she began, and stopped. They heard feet on the stairs. John Halley came in from the hall, smiling. The smile creased a long brown face. He wore a dinner jacket.

For a host minutes late to his own party, John Halley was unperturbed. It occurred to Lynn, smiling a guestly smile, that it probably had been many years since John Halley had been perturbed, ill at ease. He said now that he was sorry, made general sounds of greeting and added, to Margaret, that he'd decided to get changed and be out of the way.

'Of course, dear,' Margaret said, and patted her husband's sleeve. 'Good old John,' Struthers Boyd said, apropos of nothing immediately apparent, and Tom Kemper said, 'Evening, sir.' Audrey Latham said nothing, but looked up into Halley's long brown face

22

and smiled very prettily, Lynn thought. Halley moved toward the bar wagon. On his way, he tapped Boyd lightly on the shoulder; said, 'Evening, Kemper;' said, 'glad you could make it, doctor,' to Brian Perry, and paused to shake his hand. At the bar, Halley said, in a lightly pleasant voice, 'Now?' Then, directed, he mixed drinks and Abner Speed passed drinks. Returning to the fire with his own, he said, 'Cheers,' and was echoed.

'To the New York State Gas and Electric Company,' Halley said, then, and, standing with his back to the fire, smiled widely. He did not, to Lynn, seem in any way—what was the word Margaret had used? 'Moody.' He seemed to be a lean, brown man in his middle years, in a dinner jacket which fitted as perfectly as his manners, and was worn as confidently. 'May it keep what strength it has,' Halley said.

He was told, by Boyd, that he was an optimist. But Margaret said, 'John! Don't even suggest it!' The others sought to look as if they understood.

'You ought to remember, doctor,' Halley said to Brian Perry. 'Of course, it doesn't matter so much in the summer.' Perry's face showed that he did remember.

'There are various theories,' Halley said, 'as to what the company uses to transmit its power. Some say it's merely string. There is a body of opinion which holds out for baling wire.' He looked around, his smile still wide.

'There is also a group which insists that the power goes off whenever there is a heavy dew. I've never felt, myself, that that was entirely fair.'

'A breeze will do it,' Struthers Boyd said. 'Just a gentle little breeze. Of course, it's the trees. But you've got a standby, haven't you, John?'

'Of sorts,' Halley said. 'Manual job. Across the road.'

'Quit scaring people,' Margaret said. 'He loves to scare people. Nothing's going to happen.' She said this with confidence...

And, some hours later, undressing in the small corner room, Lynn thought that, as usual, Margaret Halley had been right. Lynn hung the long dinner dress (which made her tall) carefully in the closet, and took off the rest of her clothes and opened a window a very little and got into bed. She switched on the electric blanket and, almost at once, was surrounded by gentle warmth. A new year had begun, and they had all drunk toasts to it. Strangers had become friends—for that little time, in that bright room. 'You're a mighty pretty girl,' Struthers Boyd, a little flushed (but only a little flushed), had told her. 'A mighty purty girl,' in dialect which had sounded fine at the moment. 'It goes like this,' Audrey Latham had said, and sung a little song—and listened to herself and said, 'or almost like that.' Then she had held out her arms to John Halley and said,

'Dance it with me, John. See how it goes,' and they had danced a few steps to her singing. To Lynn's ears it had gone well—oh, very well.

But everything had gone well. The Halleys could be proud of their party. At midnight, Abner Speed and his wife—who was ample and wore an apron—had come into the bright room and drunk with the rest to the New Year in champagne Lynn knew was admirable, since everything else had been so admirable and so gay. They had all danced and Brian Perry, somewhat unexpectedly, had danced beautifully—much better than Mr Boyd, who could not really be said to have danced at all. (But that had been fun, too. All of it had been fun.) Toward the end, she thought, John Halley had grown a little tired; he had sat and watched, sipping scotch and water, as he had done all evening; saying little. He was older, of course—but probably not older than Struthers Boyd. And Boyd had certainly neither sat, nor said nothing. 'The classmate type.' Lynn smiled to herself in the darkness. How aptly Margaret had hit it off. How nice everyone was. How—how *bright* the world was. Even a year ago, although by then she had been much better, she had been still a little afraid of brightness.

And Brian Perry had kissed her. Of course, it had meant nothing. On New Year's Eve, after the toasts, people kiss people—kiss the person they are nearest to. Chance governed that—

25

Margaret and Tom Kemper had kissed, since they were standing side by side. And even John Halley and Audrey. (Struthers Boyd had kissed all of the women, and shaken hands firmly with the other men. But that, too, went without saying.) It had been merely one of those accidents of placing that, when the New Year began, Brian had been standing beside her, smiling down at her. (Down! Think of that!) So, he would have been a boor not to kiss her, and he was certainly not a boor. He was... it had all been...

It would be fun tomorrow—and next week—to think back to the party; sort out the pleasant details of what was now only a remembered gentle blow. But now it would be most fun of all to sleep, warm and secure in bed, afraid no longer of anything—not of the storm outside, not of anything. He had had to stoop to kiss her, and his lips had been firm on hers and for an instant (since he was not a boor) he had drawn her to him—and—and...

She fought against awakening; fought to regain the soft warmth of sleep. Not yet awake, she pulled the blanket closer under her chin; sleeping still, she pulled her knees up so that, lying on her side, her long body was curled, as nearly as possible as a cat curls. She began to dream of ice—ice moving down on her, slowly and relentlessly, as a glacier moves. She awoke, and was shivering. For a moment she could not remember where she was, and then remembered. At the Halleys', in a corner guestroom. She must, sleeping uneasily (but not for a long time had she slept so), have thrown the covers off. She must—

Then she remembered more. An electric blanket—was she afraid of an electric blanket? The blanket should be warm. Or, had she forgotten to turn it on? That was not it surely; warmth had come quickly when she was first in bed, pressing palms together with the blanket between them. There was no warmth in the blanket.

She reached out to the control on the table beside the bed. She had moved the control clockwise to turn the blanket on. Had she, somehow in her sleep, turned it off again or, be coming too warm, turned it down too far? She twisted the knob of the dial; first counterclockwise to turn the current off, then back again—far back. She waited. The blanket remained cold.

Something had happened to the blanket. Something was always (in her experience) happening to automatic things. Mysteriously, for wayward reasons of their own, they ceased to be automatic, just when you most needed them. She would have to get up now and get her coat out of the closet, and put it on top of the blanket; she would have to close the window and sleep in a stuffy room. She would have—

A small red light began to glow on the table

beside the bed. For a moment she did not recognize it. Then she did—as the indicator light on the blanket control. The thing had turned itself on again. Electricity was beyond comprehension. Almost at once the blanket began to grow warm.

Slowly, tentatively, she stretched out her long, slim legs. Already it was warm, even at the foot of the bed. That was a nice thing about them, when they worked. They worked all over ...

Brian Perry's lips had been warm on hers. He must, without those rimless glasses—there is something so harsh about rimless glasses—he must be—he's not more than forty or so, I shouldn't think—he was married, but his wife is dead—what was his wife's name? I wonder if ...

She slept, having never been quite awake.

CHAPTER THREE

She was awakened by the sound of voices, the sounds of people hurrying in the house. Someone ran on bare flooring. She looked at her watch, and found it was only a little after eight. That was early, surely, for the morning of New Year's Day. She could not, lying still in bed, under the electric blanket, make out words. She thought the voices were those of two, perhaps three, of the men. Then she heard someone—Dr Perry?—say, *'In here,'* and realized that he must be speaking quite loudly. She heard the sound of a door closing.

Something had gone wrong. There was wrongness in all the sounds—a hurrying excitement. Lynn Ross got out of bed, was aware of a sudden tenseness in her body and in her mind. She closed the window. Snow still was falling, but not, she thought, as heavily as it had fallen the night before, had been falling when she went to bed. Shivering in the cold room, she went to the closet and got a woolen robe she had hung there. She belted the robe tight about her, and went to the bedroom door. Warmth came in from the hall as she opened the door.

A little way along the hall, nearer the stairs, Audrey Latham was standing, her slight body rigid, her entire attitude one of intent listening. She wore a sweater and slacks. She turned, quickly, when Lynn opened her door and stepped into the hall.

'Something's happened,' the slim blond girl said. 'Something terrible's happened.' As she spoke she moved toward the stairs. As she reached the top of the flight, she put a hand on the stair rail, steadying herself. *'John,'* she said. *'I think it's something about John.'* She started down the stairs, moving slowly, holding to the rail. Lynn hesitated for a moment, then followed her.

They were half way down the stairs, Lynn standing a few steps above Audrey Latham, when Brian Perry came from the living room into the hall and looked up at them.

'There's nothing you can do,' he said. 'Nothing anybody can.'

'What is it?' Audrey said. '*What is it?*'

'Halley,' Brian Perry said. 'He's dead, Miss Latham. Somehow—God knows how—he got into the lake. We found him a little while ago.'

Perry moved under the stairs. They could hear him lift a telephone receiver, whirl the dial. 'I want the police,' Perry said. 'The State police, I suppose. I have to report an accidental death.' There was a momentary pause. 'I'll hold on,' he said, and at the same moment Audrey Latham gave a little, shuddering cry, and swayed where she stood, holding to the stair rail. Lynn reached her, and held her. The girl's slight body was shaking.

'John,' she said. 'He said—*John!*'

'Yes,' Lynn said.

Margaret came out of the living room into the hall. She was white. Even her lips were colorless, and she looked many years older than she had looked the night before—had looked in the soft light from the lamps, from the flickering fire. She looked up at the two on the stairs, and for an instant as if she did not recognize them. Then she said, 'John is dead.' Her voice had a thin quality, but it was steady. 'He drowned himself,' she said. 'Went down to

30

the lake and drowned himself.'

'Margaret!' Lynn said. She released Audrey Latham, who clung to the rail, who stared down at Margaret Halley. Lynn started down toward the small woman who looked up at them with so fixed an expression.

'You let him,' Audrey said. 'You *let* him. You knew—you said you knew. *And you didn't do anything!*'

'No,' Margaret Halley said, in a voice without expression. 'No, I didn't do enough.'

'The Halley house,' Brian Perry said. 'On Lake Carabec. We found Mr Halley in the lake this morning. He slipped, apparently. Struck his head on something. Drowned.' His voice stopped for a moment. 'Several hours,' he said, and then, 'Perry. Brian Perry. I'm a doctor, sergeant.' He listened once more. 'No,' he said. 'It won't do any good. He's been dead for hours, as I said.'

He hung up the telephone. He came out into the hall and went to Margaret Halley.

'As soon as they can get through,' he said. He looked up at Lynn and Audrey Latham. 'It was an accident,' he said.

Margaret Halley shook her head. The movement was slow, almost methodical.

'It's no good,' she said. 'You know what it was, Brian. What I was afraid of. What we always have to be afraid of and—and try to guard against.'

'I don't know,' Perry said. 'You did what
31

you could. All anybody could do. There's nothing now but to wait. We'd better have some coffee, Margaret.'

'Of course,' Margaret Halley said, in the same thin voice. 'Tell them, will you, Brian?' And then she started up the stairs. The two standing there drew aside to let her pass. But she stopped, level with them. Margaret spoke, but only to Audrey Latham.

'I blame myself,' she said. 'Quite as much as you could wish, Miss Latham. As even you could wish.'

And then, her set face white, she went on up the stairs. She went up and they could hear her steps, steady, unhurried—in an odd fashion resolute—on the flooring of the upper hall.

'Isn't there something—' Lynn said, and Brian Perry shook his head.

'Nothing, Miss Ross,' he said. 'Come down and we'll have coffee. Miss Latham?'

But Audrey Latham seemed not to hear him. She brushed past Lynn and ran up the stairs, ran the few feet along the hall which took her to the room in which she had slept. The door closed, sharply, behind her.

The dining room was across the central hall from the living room. Brian Perry, very tall indeed in slacks and a sweater over a woolen shirt, led Lynn Ross into it, and through it to a smaller room beyond. There, Tom Kemper and Struthers Boyd sat with cigarettes, coffee cups in front of them. Kemper was dressed much as Brian Perry was. He said, 'Good morning, Miss Ross,' in a low, grave voice. 'This is a terrible thing that's happened.' Boyd wore a bathrobe which, when Lynn and Perry entered, he tightened around him. His heavy face was pale, now, and unshaven. It seemed to sag. He rubbed a hand along his face.

'Old John,' Boyd said. 'Hard to believe it.' He rubbed his face again. 'Feel like hell about it,' he said. 'Why would he do a thing like that? God—I feel like hell.'

He seemed to include, this time, more in the statement than he had before. He pressed his hands against his forehead.

'You get them, doctor?' he said.

'They,' Brian Perry told him, were on their way. Because of the condition of the roads, it might take them time. Boyd stood up. He said, in a voice which drooped as his face drooped, that he'd better get some clothes on. He looked at Kemper; looked down at Kemper's legs. Lynn looked too. Kemper's slacks were wet to the knees. 'If I were you,' Boyd said, 'I'd get something dry on.'

'He's right,' Perry said. 'Getting pneumonia won't help anybody.'

Reminded, Kemper shivered; said, 'Hell yes.' He went out of the small breakfast room and Boyd went after him. Brian Perry touched a bell, and Lucinda Speed peered into the room through a partly opened door. She shook her head and sighed; and Brian Perry asked if they

33

could have some coffee. She said, 'I'll get it,' and the door closed.

'Kemper got him out,' Brian Perry said. He looked across the table at Lynn. He took his rimless glasses off and his eyes seemed larger without the glasses. He laid the glasses on the table beside his plate. 'He wasn't far from the bank, but Kemper had to wade in to get him.'

'It's so dreadful,' Lynn said. 'After last night. We—we were all drinking to the New Year.' She discovered that her voice shook. Unexpectedly, Brian Perry reached across the table and, briefly, put one of his hands over one of hers. He had long hands, with very long fingers. He did not, otherwise, respond to what she had said.

'Apparently,' Perry said, 'he went down to the lake for something—or to the boathouse for something. Before he went to bed. He'd put on the outdoor shoes he kept downstairs. Somehow he lost his footing in the snow and fell into the water. He hit his head on something. A rock, probably. That stunned him.'

'It was—it's clear what happened?'

'I'd think so,' he said. 'John could have stood up and the water wouldn't have been higher than his waist.'

'But the way Margaret talked—' Lynn said. Mrs Speed came in, carrying a tray. She poured them coffee, indicated toast wrapped in a napkin. She sighed deeply and went out again.

34

'Yes,' Brian Perry said. 'She thinks he killed himself.' He hesitated for a moment. 'He was in a depression, Margaret says. As a matter of fact—' He broke off. 'But that doesn't matter, now,' he said. 'A person in a depression is very likely to try suicide. Part of the treatment is to prevent suicide. It's possible that—'

'I tried to kill myself a year ago—a little over a year ago,' Lynn said, quite steadily. 'The world was—all gray. Formless. I took too many sleeping pills. And—now I'm all right.'

He put his glasses on, and looked at her with care—looked at her, she thought, professionally. He took his glasses off again.

'You're quite all right,' he said. 'You went to Margaret?' She nodded. 'She's very good. She was probably right about her husband. Of course, in a close relationship, it's hard to keep perspective. She wanted me to talk to John, if he was willing. See if I agreed. Better drink your coffee, Miss Ross. And—here.' He pushed the plate of toast nearer. She looked at it. 'Yes,' he said. She took a piece of toast. It was wrong to be hungry. Nevertheless, she was hungry.

Margaret had, he told her, sipping his own coffee, been worried for some time about her husband's state of mind. Toward the end of the party the night before she had become afraid that Halley was entering the depressive phase. She had tried, after the others had gone up, to get him to go to bed, but he had not been ready.

35

She had left him sitting by the fire.

'She went into his room early, to make sure he was all right. She found he wasn't there. She went downstairs and found he wasn't there, either. Then she called Kemper. Kemper got me up.'

They had convinced themselves that John Halley was not in the house, and then had gone out into the snow. In the snow they had found soft depressions, almost filled—faint hollows in the surface, just perceptible; only possibly what remained of tracks made in the snow hours before. They followed the faint marks—to the boathouse, to Halley's body. He had been dead for several hours. They had carried his body back to the house.

'She must be right,' Lynn said, after a longish pause. Brian was lighting a cigarette. He let the match burn down. At the last instant, he shook the match out. 'Margaret, I mean,' Lynn said. 'Why would he go there, except—except to do what she thinks?'

Brian Perry struck another match. He lighted his cigarette, this time. Then, belatedly, he pushed the pack toward Lynn. He leaned across the table, with still another match flickering. He said, 'Sorry,' and held the match to her cigarette. Then he said, 'I don't know, Miss Ross. It is, I'll have to admit, a little complicated. But I'm quite sure he slipped, struck his head, and lost consciousness. And that—'

36

Outside, but very close, there was, briefly, the sound of a siren.

'They made good time,' Brian Perry said, and stood up. He walked out of the breakfast room and through the larger room beyond— the now rather dreary room in which, last night, they had dined with candles on the table. Lynn, finishing her coffee, and her cigarette, heard the voices of men from the hall. After a time, the voices ceased and she heard the front door close. They had—she supposed they had—gone down to the lake.

There was no one in the hall when she went into it; there might, from the silence, have been no one else in the house. She went up the stairs slowly, and toward her room. She reached the door of what, she knew now, was Audrey Latham's room. She heard a voice behind the door—a level voice, Margaret Halley's voice.

'—will do no good to anyone,' Margaret Halley said. 'I'm sure you will agree to that, Miss Latham. No possible good. Merely add needless unpleasantness to what—'

'Leave me alone,' Audrey said, and her voice rose, sounded close to hysteria. 'You think I don't know about you and—'

Lynn had, involuntarily, hesitated when she heard Margaret speaking. Now she went on— quickly but as quietly as she could, so that the two behind the door would not have the embarrassment of realizing that they might have been overheard. She closed the door of

37

her room behind her, softly. It was still cold in the room. The little indicator light of the blanket still showed red. She had forgotten to turn it off. She turned it off, and shivered in the chill of the room. She went into the bathroom and found it warmer, and let water run and found it hot. She showered, then, in water as hot as she could stand, and afterward dressed in a warm sweater and slacks.

What do I do now? she wondered. What can I do? She had planned, after she had changed, to go to Margaret Halley; to offer to do whatever she could do. But there had been something in Margaret's voice, heard through the closed door—a quality which made her sure that, whatever Margaret felt, it would be useless, almost an impertinence, to go to her with conventional words.

The 'dark year' had left, somewhere deep in her mind, a tiny shadow of its darkness: a dread of indecision. Standing now in the center of the small room, that dread for an instant grew larger. What do I do? I must *decide* what to do. But she looked at the small darkness and it vanished. This was not the same; not in the least the same. There were not now, in a real sense, alternatives to choose between. Since she could do nothing, it did not really matter what she did. She chose, therefore, and simply, to go where it would be warmer.

She went out of her room and along the hall toward the stairway. Tom Kemper came toward her. He had changed to a dark suit. He said, 'I was looking for Margaret. Do you know where she is?' And then, 'Somebody ought to be with her.'

'She was with Miss Latham a little while ago,' Lynn said. 'I heard her voice. In Miss Latham's room.'

'Why the—' Kemper began, and his youthful, open face was briefly knotted in an expression Lynn could not interpret. 'That's all right, then,' he said. 'This is awful, isn't it?'

She nodded her head. There was no point in adding one meaningless word to another.

He half smiled.

'Aside from everything else,' he said. 'Of course it is a hell of a sad thing—a tragic thing. Aside from that, I mean. I feel a lot in the way. Don't you?'

That was how Lynn did feel. It was a trivial way to feel, an inappropriate way. The human mind is by no means always equal to the tragic.

'That's exactly how I feel,' Lynn said. 'As if—well, as if I ought to go back to New York. Just—disappear.'

'Get out from under foot,' Kemper said. 'That's it. But—I suppose we can't do that. Not right away.' He paused, then came on toward her. 'The police have got here,' he said. 'A trooper. Gone down to the lake, with the doctor. They have to check up on things like this, you know. Accidents. Or—' He did not finish.

'Suicide,' Lynn said. 'Margaret thinks Mr Halley killed himself.'

'I know,' Kemper said. 'I'm afraid maybe she's right. The poor old guy had these—these spells. Times when he got very down. Margaret's been afraid for a long time that—well, that something like this would happen.'

'If the police think that, they'll want to ask questions, won't they?' she said. 'Whether any of us noticed anything? Whether he said anything? Find out what we know before we leave?'

'I suppose so,' Kemper said. 'It oughtn't to take long.' He smiled again, faintly. 'No use standing here, is there?' he said, and motioned to the staircase. They went down into the entrance hall. It was empty. The double doors to the living room were closed. They went into the cheerless dining room. Kemper went to a window. He said the snow seemed to be about over. Then he said, 'Here they come,' and Lynn joined him at the window.

A uniformed trooper was coming toward the house, wading slowly through deep snow. Dr Brian Perry was with him. They came up on the porch and stamped their feet. At the window, Lynn could hear the front door open. 'I'll ask her to come down,' Brian Perry said, and they could hear him going up the stairs. The trooper came to the door of the dining room, and looked at Lynn and Tom Kemper. He was very young, Lynn thought. He said, 'Good

40

morning,' in a pleasant voice. He said, 'My name's Crowley. Trooper Crowley.' He waited, politely.

Lynn told him who she was. Kemper said he was Thomas Kemper.

'It's a bad business,' Crowley said. 'Very bad for everybody.'

'Did he—' Lynn began, and the young trooper shook his head.

'Don't know much about it,' he said. 'Could have been an accident. But why was he down there? Could have been suicide. But why do it the hard way?' He looked at them. 'I suppose neither of you knows the answers?'

'How could we?' Kemper said.

'That's right,' the trooper said. 'Well, be somebody else along, probably. Detective captain, most likely.'

'I gather,' Kemper said, 'we wait till he comes?'

'Wish you would,' Trooper Crowley said. 'Might be something he'd want to ask you. Quite a snow, wasn't it?'

He seemed very young indeed. He seemed to be making conversation, and looked from one to the other. Kemper said it had been quite a snow.

'Have the plows through pretty soon,' the trooper said. 'Well—' He went out of the room, then. He closed the door behind him.

*　　*　　*

Captain M. L. Heimrich, criminal identification division, New York State Police, was sound asleep. Then he was wide awake. There was no transition. Captain Heimrich, lying in bed in his room at the Old Stone Inn, Van Brunt (Town of Van Brunt, County of Putnam) looked at his watch, and was somewhat surprised. It showed him the time was ten twenty-five. No, ten twenty-seven. It had been years since he had slept so late. He could not remember when he had slept so late.

But it had been years, also, since he had taken a young woman out for New Year's Eve. The one thing had led to the other, naturally. Heimrich sat up in bed and lighted a cigarette, carrying the unusual one step further. He did not, normally, smoke before breakfast. He seemed to be walking new paths.

It had been a pleasant evening. It had been one of the pleasantest evenings he could recall. He was still somewhat surprised that he had brought himself to embark upon it. He was an old dog, learning new tricks.

It had started with a notice, to its customers, from the Old Stone Inn of Van Brunt. As was its custom, the Inn had announced, there would be a special New Year's Eve dinner. Dinner would be followed by dancing. Only forty reservations were to be accepted, so that such prized guests as Captain M. L. Heimrich would find the inn uncrowded. The Inn hoped that the valued guest to whom this invitation was directed, would make his reservation in good time, thus securing a table advantageously placed.

Heimrich had received this invitation some days before Christmas, at the Hawthorne Barracks of the State police. He had folded it neatly and placed it in a wastebasket. Some little time later he had taken it out, and unfolded it carefully, and read it again, with the thought that the Inn must be more or less scraping the bottom of its barrel of valued guests. Heimrich had stayed there for a few hot summer days during the investigation of the murder of the late supervisor of the Town of Van Brunt. He had not had, particularly, the sense of being valued. Over the whole incident, he had thought, the Inn, together with the rest of Van Brunt, would have preferred that a veil be drawn.

Heimrich had folded the invitation again, with the same care, but this time had put it in his pocket. Being a deliberate man, he had thought matters over for the rest of that day, and for most of the next. The matters he thought of appeared, at first, ridiculous. He was old for this sort of thing. A young woman like Susan Faye—a slender gray-eyed young woman, with square shoulders and other seemly attributes—would long since have planned for the holidays. In Van Brunt, and its environs, there were doubtless many young men of her own age who would be delighted to take Susan Faye to the special dinner (to be followed by dancing) at the Old Stone Inn. He—he must be fifteen years older than she. Perhaps even a year or two in excess of fifteen. He would be making himself ridiculous. He was anything but a dancing man.

'Why—hullo, captain,' Susan Faye had said, when she answered her telephone. It had been absurd of him to find her voice exciting.

She had been very well. Yes, young Michael had also been very well. The Colonel had eaten something which had disagreed with him, but was now, also, in admirable health.

'Is he still as sad as always?' Heimrich asked.

'He seems to be,' Susan Faye said, in her grave young voice, and did not hurry Captain Heimrich.

'Naturally,' Heimrich said then, apropos of nothing in particular. 'Mrs Faye, I wondered whether by any chance you—'

She heard him through, which, as he spoke, he felt to be more than he deserved.

'I'd like to very much,' Susan had said. 'There is nothing I'd like better, Merton.'

Captain Heimrich, who had always regarded his given name with dogged disapproval, found that it sounded pleasantly in his ears.

At three minutes after midnight Heimrich, putting down the glass from which he had drunk a toast to the New Year, found that Susan Faye, sitting beside him on the

44

banquette, was looking up at him, as if there were still something to be expected. For a moment, Heimrich had been at a loss, and then he remembered. Somewhat to his astonishment, and greatly to his enjoyment, Captain Heimrich had kissed the sweet, wide mouth of Mrs Susan Faye, widow, mother of a boy of seven (and a half, by now) and custodian of the largest of Great Danes. Leaving her at her home some time later, Heimrich had kissed her again. He had driven back to the inn through heavy snow, and had been quite unconscious of the fact that dangling links on one of the tire chains were banging angrily against the fender.

Heimrich, who was a very solid man, with a brown face which might have been carved from some durable wood, got out of bed. He wore dark blue pajamas. He went into the bathroom, and ran a tub, since there was no shower. He had one foot in it when the telephone rang. He had a momentary feeling of pleased expectancy, which was, again, ridiculous. He said, 'Heimrich speaking,' wished for the briefest of instants that he had used other words, and discovered that he had not needed to.

'Yes, Charlie,' he said, to Sergeant Charles Forniss, speaking from Hawthorne. 'Yes, I was awake.'

'Young Crowley,' Forniss said. 'Trooper Ray Crowley?'

45

'Yes,' Heimrich said. 'I remember Crowley.'

'Just phoned in,' Forniss said. 'Answered a squeal from up around Lake Carabec. Man named Halley—John Halley. Found in the lake. Wife says it's suicide. Says she was afraid he might. Man had been in a depression.'

'Crowley doesn't like it? Say why?'

'Halley had to walk a hundred yards, through pretty deep snow. Jump in a very cold lake.'

'Well?'

'There was a bottle of sleeping pills on the bed table in his room. All of them he would have needed.'

'All right,' Captain Heimrich said. 'I'll pick you up, Charlie.'

CHAPTER FOUR

The police car moved with slowness appropriate to the surface. The plow had been through on the road around Lake Carabec, but the thin packed snow it had left behind was very slippery. A link of one of the tire chains continued a rhythmic assault on the under side of the fender. Snow still was falling, but now very lightly.

Where the road came closest to the lake, was separated from it only by an ancient wooden rail and a pitching bank, Sergeant Forniss drove with particular care. At one place, where the road curved sharply in toward the water, part of the rail was down. Something had hit the rail and scarred it, so that unweathered wood showed.

'Somebody had a narrow squeak there,' Heimrich said. To this, Sergeant Forniss said, 'Yep. Looks like it.' They came to a driveway and turned up it. Here the plow had not been, but there were ruts in the snow. They followed the ruts until they came to a police car, parked so that it obstructed entrance to, or exit from, a three-car garage. Forniss pulled up beside it.

'Ambulance been and gone,' Forniss said, indicating the broad, deep tracks of a vehicle with chains. 'But they'd moved the body anyway.'

'Yes,' Heimrich said. 'They had to, of course.'

The door opened and a young trooper came out. Heimrich said, 'Morning, Ray. Had another hunch?'

Trooper Ray Crowley flushed. He looked younger than ever. He said it could be he was nuts. He said there wasn't much of anything to go on, and the more he heard about it, the more he thought maybe he *was* nuts.

'But?' Heimrich said.

'Why would a man go out and jump in a cold lake?' Crowley said. 'Do it the hard way? Only—his wife says he's tried several times to kill himself. Says he was in a depression. And—

47

seems she ought to know, being a doctor. Psychiatrist. Also, she says there's no telling *how* somebody will go about killing himself.' He paused. 'Guess maybe I shouldn't have bothered you, sir,' he said. 'On a hunch, like you say.'

'Well,' Heimrich said. 'You did, Ray. And— the water must have been very cold. Not like a nice warm garage, with the motor running.'

'Or sleeping pills,' Ray Crowley said. 'Half full bottle in his room. Nembutal, his wife says. She prescribed it. That would have been the easy way.' He looked at Heimrich and Sergeant Forniss. 'And then,' he said, 'maybe it was just an accident. Only—'

Heimrich waited.

'You want to see where it happened, captain?' Crowley asked. 'Or talk to them first?' He gestured toward the house.

'Oh, at the beginning,' Heimrich said. 'The end, rather. Where was it, Crowley?'

Crowley led them through the snow, in an area where there had already been much walking in the snow. He led them down to the road, and across it, and then down a sharp slope. There was a small building at the edge of the water.

'Boathouse,' Crowley said. 'No boat in it, they say. Here's where they say it was.'

Near the boathouse, the snow was much trampled down to the water. There was a rimming of ice on the lake, and there it had

48

been broken. (And was now beginning to freeze again.) Something had been dragged through the snow.

'This way when I got here,' Crowley said. 'But, you can't blame them for getting him out, I guess.'

'No,' Heimrich said. He ventured into the trampled area, moving carefully. He slipped and caught himself. 'Rock on the surface here,' he said. 'Very slippery with the snow on it, naturally. How deep's the water, Ray? Here at the edge.'

'Three or four feet. According to a man named Perry—he's a doctor, too—Halley hit his head on something. Knocked himself out, Dr Perry thinks. As a matter of fact, Dr Perry thinks it was an accident. Only—what was he doing down here?' He paused. 'Of course,' he said, 'there'd been a party.'

'Yes,' Heimrich said. 'I supposed there had. He may have been a little drunk. Come out for fresh air—or just to see if it was still snowing—or for any other reason a man who's a little drunk has for doing things.'

'They say he wasn't drunk. His wife says that. Dr Perry says that.'

Captain Heimrich said, 'Hm-m,' and came back up the bank, using considerable care. He stood and looked around; looked across the lake. 'Pretty here in the summer,' he said. 'Always liked Carabec.'

He continued to look around—at the

49

trodden snow by the bank, out of the water. Far out, briefly, a stretch of water caught sunlight. 'Breaking up,' Heimrich said. 'It'll get colder, now.' He looked at the boathouse, long and low. The snow had drifted at the end farther from the water. 'No boat, you say?' he said, to Ray Crowley. Crowley said that was what they told him. 'No night for a boat ride anyway,' Heimrich said.

Three heavy wires, neatly spaced, went into the boathouse, coming down to it from a pole. The wires, supported by two more poles, went up to the house on the other side of the road. 'Must have a lathe or something in there,' Heimrich said. 'Wouldn't you think, Charlie?'

Charles Forniss said, 'Yep.'

'Seem to have come right to it,' Heimrich said. 'The ones who found him, naturally. What did they say about that, Ray?'

They had said, Ray told him, that there were shallow depressions in the snow. Not tracks, in a real sense, but what remained of tracks after blowing snow had almost filled them. A man named Kemper—Thomas Kemper—had noticed them. He and Dr Perry had followed them.

Heimrich nodded. He looked again toward the boathouse, and the unmarked snow around it. 'Snowed hard until an hour or so ago, didn't it?' he said. 'Three hours after they saw these hollows. Maybe more than three hours. But nobody would come down to run a lathe either, you wouldn't think.'

'There'd still be some marks,' Forniss said.

'Now Charlie,' Heimrich said. 'Depends, doesn't it? On the wind, for one thing. Well—'

They went back the way they had come, and on the porch of the Halley house they stamped snow from their feet. A tall thin man with glasses opened the door.

'This is Captain Heimrich, doctor,' Crowley said. 'And Sergeant Forniss.'

'We were waiting for you,' Brian Perry said. 'They've taken John's body. Autopsy, I imagine?'

'Matter of routine,' Heimrich said. 'We won't bother you people long, I hope.'

'He drowned,' Brian Perry said. 'Head injury, but that was superficial.'

He stepped away from the door, and they went in, Heimrich first. Perry led them into a long living room. A charred log was all that remained of the cheerful fire of the night before, but the room was warm. There was a dust cover on one long sofa. Heimrich looked at it.

'Wet,' Perry said. 'We put him there. Mrs Halley will be down in a minute.' He looked at Heimrich, then at Forniss. 'She thinks he killed himself, you know,' he said. 'Blames herself for that. But it does happen, in spite of all we can do.' Perry shook his head slowly. 'Come down to it,' he said, 'we don't know too much. Looking at him, I wouldn't—'

51

He broke off, at the sound of footsteps on the stairs. Heimrich watched a trimly built—delicately built—woman come into the room. She was, he guessed, in her forties. She was very pale. She had not, he thought, been crying. She said, in a voice without emphasis, that they were from the police. Perry told Margaret Halley the names of the policemen.

'I'm sorry we have to—' Heimrich began, and was interrupted. Margaret Halley quite realized what they had to do.

'I know the rules,' she said. 'I'm a physician, captain. One gets used to rules. And—other things. Even to sudden death.'

She did not reveal a great deal, Heimrich thought. Except that she was under stress.

'He killed himself,' Margaret Halley said.

'Why?' Heimrich asked her.

'He was sick,' she said. 'Mentally sick. Manic-depressive psychosis. I'd thought he was improving but—it isn't always easy to tell. Sometimes not even possible. Dr Perry will tell you that.'

Heimrich looked at Perry, and Perry nodded.

'He didn't leave a note?' Heimrich said.

'He didn't,' Margaret said. 'I wouldn't have expected him to. You see—it is difficult to explain to a normal person, captain—they get to feeling that nothing matters at all. Not even explaining oneself, which is almost the last thing to go. With anyone.'

'He was depressed last night?'

Margaret Halley looked at Perry, as if she expected him to answer that. But he merely waited. His face showed very little expression, and the rimless glasses, catching lamplight, hid his eyes.

'Toward the end,' Margaret said. 'You didn't notice it, Brian?'

'He became quieter late in the party,' Brian Perry said. 'It's quite possible a depressive phase was beginning. But—I wasn't attempting diagnosis. I was—' He paused for an instant. 'Having a good time.'

She nodded to that. She said that, after the others had gone up to bed she had sat for a few minutes with her husband, in front of the fire. She had tried to talk about the party, but he had answered very briefly, without interest. She had said that she was sleepy, was going up to bed, and he had looked into the fire, and merely nodded. She had urged him to go to bed, and to that he had said, politely enough but from far away, 'Presently. Presently, my dear.' She had asked him if he wanted his usual milk and rum punch and, when he said neither yes nor no to that, had gone to the kitchen, and warmed milk in a saucepan, and poured it into a glass, added rum and bitters and taken it to him. He had nodded, and she had set it down on a table within reach. 'He didn't drink it,' she said. She had left him there. And that, she said now, had been a mistake.

'I was tired,' she said. 'Let down, with the party over. All I wanted was to get to sleep. I blame myself for that, captain. I—I feel that I failed. As a person. As a physician.'

Perry seemed about to speak. She said, 'It's no use, Brian.'

'Dr Perry,' Heimrich said. 'This head injury. Was it enough to make him lose consciousness?'

'Yes,' Perry said. 'Probably. As a matter of fact, I think it did. I think he slipped, struck his head, and drowned while he was unconscious. I've told Dr Halley that.'

'In other words, that it was an accident?'

'Yes.'

'Yes,' Heimrich said. 'It would look like that to me, naturally.'

He looked at Mrs Halley, and she shook her head. Her expression did not change.

'Why would he go down to the lake?' Heimrich said. 'If he wanted to kill himself, there must have been easier ways. Sleeping tablets, for example? They were available, I understand?'

She said, 'Yes. Oh yes,' but spoke impatiently.

'You don't understand,' she said. 'There's no reason you should. But—the lake was part of it. At the center of it.' She looked at Brian Perry. She spoke very slowly. She said, 'You realize that, Brian.'

Brian Perry merely looked at her. The

54

glasses still hid the expression in his eyes.

*   *   *

Lynn had waited a long time in the breakfast room which was behind the dining room in the Halley house. At first, Tom Kemper had been with her. Then, after some time, Struthers Boyd had come into the room and complained about a headache. At first, she had watched the snow falling beyond the windows. Then the snow stopped and, after a time, the sun showed itself periodically. The snow on the ground would glitter in sunlight. Then dark shadows would hurry across it. Lucinda Speed came in twice from the kitchen into the small room, and brought fresh coffee. She sniffled when she entered, and sighed deeply when she left, and as she poured coffee for them she shook her head dolefully from side to side. Mrs Speed, Lynn Ross thought, was equal to the occasion.

Lynn did not, herself, feel adequate to it. What had happened was shocking; it was especially shocking under the circumstances—a party weekend changed suddenly into hopeless dreariness. Yet not, for her, turned into tragedy, even in the commonest, which was the most exaggerated, use of the word. Not, at any rate, into tragedy to be felt as such. She was sorry that John Halley had killed himself; shocked that he had; saddened for Margaret. But it would have been

55

unreasonable to expect that she, Lynn Ross, should feel that sense of loss which turns the shocking into the shattering. She had, most simply, hardly known John Halley.

She told herself this, and yet thought that she should feel more deeply about what had happened—feel something other than a gritty emptiness, a kind of disappointment.

But if she was not equal to the situation, as Mrs Speed so clearly was, it seemed to her that Tom Kemper was even less so. When she had first met him she had thought, 'How cheerful he is,' and, now that cheerfulness was obviously out of the question, she looked at him again and could not think anything at all about him. A youngish man, of medium height, with a rather square face and rather regular features, with lines to show that he smiled a good deal. He maintained an expression of gravity, or, she supposed, an expression so intended. The trouble, she thought, was that gravity was an attitude unfamiliar to Kemper, and one in which he felt insecure. The situation, she thought, was one requiring more maturity than Tom Kemper had achieved. Or, it appeared, than she had either.

She and Kemper had remained in the dining room for only a few minutes after the young trooper had closed the door on them. Then Kemper had said he could use more coffee, and to this she had nodded agreement. They had gone to the breakfast room and Kemper—who clearly knew the house better than she did, which was after all not at all—had gone into the kitchen and come back to say that Mrs Speed was seeing to it.

The coffee had come, and they had drunk it, and smoked, and talked little. Kemper had said, from a window, that it seemed to be slackening off. He said, again, that he wished they could all get out from under foot. Then he had sat, looking fixedly at his coffee cup, with his expression of gravity in place. Lynn had gone, in turn, to look out the window, and had stayed there for a considerable time—until, in fact, Struthers Boyd had come in and had said, 'God! This is awful,' but whether about what had happened or his own headache, which he subsequently mentioned from time to time, was not clear.

They heard sounds from the front of the house—sounds of several men moving around—and then they heard a heavy motor running, and racing, as if a car were having trouble in the snow. At these sounds, they looked toward them, and then, when the sounds led to nothing, away again. 'Hope they haven't forgotten they've got us here,' Kemper said, some time later. After that, he went again to the kitchen, carrying the empty coffee pot. He returned with the pot filled.

It was a little after noon that they heard the door from the entrance hall into the dining room open and close again. The young trooper came through the dining room. Inside the door of the breakfast room, he said that he was sorry they had been kept waiting. He said that, if Mr Kemper didn't mind, Captain Heimrich would like to talk to him for a few minutes.

'Don't know what I can tell him,' Kemper said. 'But, sure, if he thinks I can.'

Kemper went with the young trooper.

'Sort of making a fuss about it, aren't they?' Boyd said. He put both hands to his head, and held it tenderly. 'Don't mean that the way it sounds,' he said. 'Sorry as hell about poor old John. All I mean is—he slipped and fell in the lake. Or, maybe, went and jumped in. Either way—he's dead, isn't he? Fussing about it won't bring him back to life.'

Lynn said she supposed the police had to find out as much as they could. 'If it's suicide,' she said, 'I suppose they have to know. Wouldn't it make a difference about—oh, insurance?'

'Doubt it,' Boyd said. 'Probably had what he's got a long time. Anyway, he wasn't a man who needed insurance, you know. That's for people like me. Not people with as much of his own as John's got. Or did have. Be Margaret's now, I suppose.'

'I don't know, then,' Lynn said. 'I suppose they have to find out, if they can. I suppose there's a law about it.'

Boyd seemed to have lost interest. He tipped

the coffee pot over his cup, and swore when only a few drops poured. He got up, apparently with an effort, and went to the kitchen. He came back to say, 'She's making it,' and to sit again, head in hands again. After a time, Mrs Speed came in once more with coffee. This time she sighed deeply, but did not sniffle.

It was about half an hour after he had taken Kemper away that Trooper Ray Crowley returned. This time he took Boyd away. Boyd groaned.

* * *

Captain Heimrich watched the large, drooping, Mr Boyd leave the living room. Captain Heimrich closed his eyes. He said, absently, that they did not seem to be getting much of any place. It was possible, Sergeant Forniss said, that there was no place to get. At that, Heimrich opened his eyes, and said, 'Now Charlie.'

'He drowned himself,' Forniss said. 'Or he had an accident. Maybe he went down to the lake to drown himself, and had an accident and fell in before he jumped in. Nothing else shows.'

'If he went to the lake to drown himself,' Heimrich said, 'why did he change his shoes? He wouldn't have been afraid of catching cold, would he, Charlie? And if he went for some other reason, what was the reason?'

Heimrich closed his eyes again, expecting no answer, and getting none that helped. ('Yep,' Forniss said, 'I see what you mean.') They had now spent some time on it, and they were much where they were when they arrived, which was much where Ray Crowley had got before he telephoned. (A smart boy, Crowley was proving himself to be. Something would have to be done about him.)

There had been, in Halley's room, a bottle half filled with capsules. Halley's failure to use them, if he wanted to kill himself, was unexplained. But Margaret Halley was sure that her husband had killed himself. She brushed aside the objection to method, but there Heimrich was not sure he followed her. 'The lake was at the center of it.' Why? How? 'It called him,' she had said, which was no explanation. 'It was deep in his subconscious,' she had said, which did not help greatly. And, after she had gone, Brian Perry had said that he did not know, precisely, what she meant, except that in some way the lake might have been a symbol in John Halley's mind. It was all entirely unsatisfactory.

There was, in the boathouse, an electric generator, installed years before when the electric lines had not reached to the far side of Lake Carabec. Since then, the generator had been kept ready to supply electricity during the power failures which were frequent in the area. The generator did not, as some did, cut in automatically when the power failed. Somebody had to go and start it. And somebody—oh yes, Boyd—remembered that Halley had mentioned the generator during the evening. For what good that did them.

It might have done considerable good. If the power had failed, Halley might have gone down to start the generator, and might have slipped and struck his head and gone into the bitter water of the lake. On hearing of the generator, Heimrich had checked at once. The power had not failed. The New York State Gas and Electric Company was quite sure of this. It was also, from the tone of its voice, a little surprised. (Heimrich learned, later, that several bitter jokesters, brooding on the past and enlivened at parties, had called to report, in accents of vast astonishment, that their power was *on*. The Company had not been much amused.)

With obstacles to two theories, it was evident that a third remained. It was that, Heimrich supposed, which made him stick at it—perhaps made him exaggerate the objections to either suicide or accident. (After all, Halley just might have gone for a walk, bad night or not; for what is called a 'breath of fresh air.' He might even, if he had been drinking, been dizzied by the fresh air.) It did not matter, in the long run, how John Halley had come to die, unless he had been murdered. There was nothing to suggest he had been.

'We may as well get on with it,' Heimrich said, opening his eyes. 'Who else have we got?'

'The other women,' Forniss said. 'The little blonde. Seems pretty upset, Crowley tells me. Didn't you, Crowley?'

'More than the others,' Crowley said. 'But—maybe she just shows it more.'

'The tall girl,' Forniss said. 'Miss—' He consulted notes. 'Lynn Ross. She's the one out ill the breakfast room. Her room's at the back of the house. Not likely she saw anything.'

'Not likely she was awake,' Heimrich said. 'However, ask her to come in, will you, Ray?'

Ray went.

'Have you got much idea what sort of man Halley was, Charlie?' Heimrich asked.

'Nope,' Forniss said.

'No,' Heimrich said. 'Neither have I.' He closed his eyes. 'It's odd, in a way,' he said.

*   *   *

There were three men in the living room, near the fireplace in which there was no fire. The young trooper in uniform; two solid men, one a little taller than the other. The taller one, Lynn thought, looked like a policeman, although she could not decide why he did. The other, a squarely built man, with a square face, and unexpectedly bright blue eyes, looked—well, like anybody. They stood up when she went into the room.

62

'My name's Heimrich, Miss Ross,' the man who did not look, particularly, like a policeman, said. 'Captain Heimrich. This is Sergeant Forniss. You've met Trooper Crowley. We're trying to find out what happened.'

'I don't know,' Lynn said. 'Except—somehow—Mr Halley was drowned. What do you want me to tell you?'

The man named Heimrich smiled faintly, and the smile changed his solid face.

'Now Miss Ross,' he said. 'I don't know, really. Anything you can. You see, Mrs Halley is afraid her husband killed himself. But it may have been an accident. We're trying to find out, for one thing, whether during the evening Mr Halley did anything, or said anything, to indicate he was depressed.'

She did not answer immediately. After she had thought, she shook her head.

'He was quiet toward the end of the party,' she said. 'But, I thought he was tired.' She hesitated. 'Actually,' she said, 'I don't know I really thought that—thought about it at all. It's just—when I remember back—' She was not being at all clear, Lynn Ross thought. She wanted to be as clear as she could.

'Yes,' Heimrich said. 'It's often like that, naturally. Did you know Mr Halley well, Miss Ross?'

'No,' she said. 'He was—well, I suppose, just Margaret's husband. I'd only met him a few

63

times. He was older, of course. Older than she. A good deal older than I am.' She hesitated. 'Mrs Halley was my physician,' she said. She did not know why she said it. It had nothing to do with anything. But Heimrich seemed, somehow, to be waiting for her to say it—to say whatever came into her mind. Why, she thought, in a way it's as it was with Margaret.

'I had a—a nervous breakdown,' Lynn said. 'People call it that. Mrs Halley—I should say Dr Halley—got me through it. Did she tell you that?'

'No,' Heimrich said. 'She has, actually, told me very little. I haven't pressed her. She's—under great strain.'

That was it, Lynn realized. Margaret showed—strain. Not grief so much. Rather a kind of tightness.

'She blames herself,' Lynn said. 'She said that to Miss Latham. As much as—' She stopped.

'Yes?' Heimrich said.

'Something about blaming herself as much as Miss Latham could want her to,' Lynn said. 'I don't know what she meant. Perhaps it was just a way of speaking.'

'Perhaps,' Heimrich said. 'So you can't think of anything about Mr Halley except that he seemed tired toward the end of the party? Tired, but not, that you noticed, particularly depressed?'

'I don't know,' she said. 'Margaret would

know. Or, Dr Perry. He's a psychiatrist too.'

'Yes,' Heimrich said. 'When you went up last night, Miss Ross. After the party?'

'Yes?'

'Mr Halley was still here? In the living room?'

'Sitting by the fire.'

'And the others?'

'Mr Kemper was still here. And Margaret, of course. I think Mr Boyd had already gone up. He'd—he'd been drinking more than the rest of us. He dozed off, woke up, said he might as well sleep in bed. He wasn't drunk at all. Just—sleepy. Sleepy and happy.'

'And Mr Halley?'

'You mean, had he been drinking a good deal? No, I shouldn't think so. We'd all had champagne, of course. It's a time when one always does. He had one long drink afterward, I think.'

'Mr Halley. Mrs Halley. Kemper. When you went up. Anyone else?'

'Dr Perry, I think. Miss Latham went up a few minutes before I did. It was a little after one. Perhaps one-thirty.'

Heimrich nodded.

'During the night,' he said. 'You didn't hear anything. A door closing, say? Or voices? Nothing wakened you?'

She shook her head.

'Nothing,' she said. 'Oh—except once. I got cold.'

Heimrich smiled at that.

'No sounds?' he said. 'You're sure it was just because you got cold? Sometimes it's hard to tell, Miss Ross.'

'Oh yes,' she said. 'I'd done something wrong about the blanket. It went off.'

'Went off?' Heimrich said, and closed his eyes for a moment. When he opened them they seemed even more brightly blue. 'You mean, it slipped off the bed?'

'No,' she said. 'It's an electric blanket. It went off—I suppose I did something wrong to it, in my sleep. Tried to turn it down or something, and turned it all the way off.'

'Do you remember doing that?'

For some reason, Lynn thought, he's not as—as easygoing as he was a minute ago.

'No,' she said. 'But it must have been that.' Wait, she thought to herself. I've got it wrong somehow. Oh—of course! 'When I waked up, because I was cold, I turned the little knob. You know? Turned it all the way off and then turned it on again. But—I had to turn it off first. I remember that.'

'And then, it came on again?'

'Not right away,' she said. 'Not—oh, for five minutes, perhaps. I was just about to get up and get a coat or something. And then it came on again.'

'Before you waked up,' Heimrich said. 'Had you been asleep long? Did you look at your watch?'

66

She shook her head, said she had not looked at her watch.

'It's hard to tell how long one's been asleep,' she said. 'But—I shouldn't think very long.' She was puzzled, now. 'You seem to think this is important,' she said. 'How could it be?'

He did not answer at once. Then he said, only, that it was hard to tell what might prove to be important.

*　　*　　*

'A circuit breaker?' Forniss said. 'Off, then on again?'

'You get a flicker,' Heimrich said. 'This would have had to be more than that. If Miss Ross is right. Ray, find out whether they've got an electric clock. See what time it is. It ought to be—' He looked at his watch—'one-fifteen, or thereabouts. You see the point, don't you, Ray?'

Ray Crowley flushed. (He was beginning to think he would never get over that habit, so inappropriate in a policeman.) He said, 'Yes sir.' Heimrich looked at him, smiled faintly, and said, 'Sorry, Ray.'

Ray left.

'Let's go out and look around, Charlie,' Heimrich said, and led the way out. From the porch, they could see most of what they needed to see.

Poles marched up the road from the south,

67

and marched away to the north. The two high-voltage lines were strung on the crossbars. A big transformer was on the pole nearest the Halley house. From it, a triple line swung up to the house, supported half way along on a private pole. And from it, also, two other sets of triple wires extended, to right and left, along the poles.

'Three on the transformer,' Forniss said.

'Yes,' Heimrich said. 'All for one and one for all. We may have to go calling.'

'Probably nobody'll be at home,' Forniss said. 'Maybe Crowley—'

They went back into the house. Crowley met them in the hall. He shook his head. He said, 'Not unless one of them brought one along. Or Lucy Speed's lying. She doesn't, that I've ever heard.'

'We'll ask,' Heimrich said. 'I shouldn't think anybody'd bring one. You checked the range, naturally? The refrigerator?'

'Yes,' Crowley said. 'Range is gas. Not automatic. No defrosting clock on the refrigerator.'

'The primitive life,' Heimrich said. 'Most of the houses along the road are closed up for the winter, probably. You'd know about that, Ray? Particularly, the houses on the same transformer box.'

Ray Crowley did know. It was part of his job to know. The Barncastles, who lived up the road—'up' was to the north—closed their house in November, each year, and had this year. The Fosters, down the road, spent winters in the city. But they had a caretaker in the house.

'Drop down and see him, Ray,' Heimrich said. 'Find out what time it is. If he has the right kind of clock.'

Ray went.

'You want this Miss Latham?' Forniss asked. Heimrich, with his eyes shut, shook his head. He said they might as well wait for Ray.

'If there's a clock,' Heimrich said. 'And if the clock's right, we'll see them all together, Charlie. Perhaps one of them will be surprised.'

Heimrich sat for a moment with his eyes closed. Then he got up and went down the long room toward a door at the rear—a door which led to the back hall and kitchen area. Forniss looked after him, and waited. Heimrich was gone only briefly.

'Checking up on young Crowley?' Forniss asked.

'On Crowley? Oh—no, Charlie. Wanted to ask Mrs Speed something. Seems Mrs Halley was right. Mrs Speed cleaned up the room this morning. Found the glass on the table, where Mrs Halley put it. Hadn't been touched, Mrs Speed says. Emptied the rum punch out and washed the glass.'

Forniss waited.

'That's all,' Heimrich said. 'Mrs Halley said her husband didn't drink the punch. I

69

supposed she meant while she was there. Now it seems he didn't drink it at all.'

Forniss nodded, slowly.

'Bears out her theory, naturally,' Heimrich said. 'For what it's worth. Wouldn't expect a man to drink a glass of warm rum punch if he'd decided to kill himself. Wouldn't seem to be in character, would it? And, apparently he didn't.'

'This Mrs Speed,' Forniss said. 'She told Mrs Halley the punch wasn't drunk?'

'Now Charlie,' Heimrich said. 'No, she says she didn't. Why should she? A little thing like that, with this dreadful thing happening? Very broken up, Mrs Speed is. Takes it hard.'

Heimrich sat down and closed his eyes. They waited, Heimrich quite relaxed, Forniss showing some tendency to prowl the room, to look out its windows. Crowley was back in some fifteen minutes. This time, he nodded as he came into the room.

'Clock in the kitchen,' he said. 'Right on the nose. And, he didn't have to set it. Makes it look—' Crowley stopped. It wasn't his job to say what things looked like.

'Yes,' Heimrich said. 'It does, Ray. Will you get them all in here? If they happen to think we're going to tell them it's all wrapped up, and that we're leaving, that will be all right. But, that isn't particularly important.'

Again Heimrich and Forniss waited. Dr Brian Perry came in first, and Lynn Ross was with him. Margaret Halley came, alone. Tom Kemper was only seconds behind her. Boyd came alone and, this time after several minutes, Audrey Latham. The slender blonde, still in slacks and a closely fitting sweater, had been crying.

'So you've got it all squared away,' Boyd said. 'Didn't take you long. I'll say that.'

Heimrich looked around at the others before he answered. Dr Perry's eyes, he thought, were narrowed behind the rimless glasses; the dark eyes of the tall Lynn Ross were merely puzzled. He could not read anything in Mrs Halley's eyes nor, and this a little surprised him, those of the well-set-up Mr Kemper. Mr Kemper had a very open countenance. He looked interested; he looked as if he were on his way to being very cheerful. Audrey Latham did not look at Heimrich, but looked, with an odd intentness, at Dr Margaret Halley. Mr Boyd appeared quite recovered from his headache. He had probably, Heimrich thought, enjoyed a hair of the dog—although, if what everyone said was true, the dog had been the merest puppy.

'Just about, Mr Boyd,' Heimrich said. 'One or two little points I thought one of you might all help me on. Comparing notes, you know? So that we can get the report accurate.' Heimrich sighed. 'They're great on accuracy,' he said. 'Want all the little details just so.' He looked around again, from one to another. 'Like times,' he said. 'They are very particular about exact times.' He sighed again, a man much put upon. (And trusted that no one would enquire, too specifically, who 'they' were. But, in his considerable experience, no one ever had.)

'It doesn't seem to matter,' Mrs Halley said. 'Why should such things matter to anybody?'

'I know,' Heimrich said. 'I'm sorry to bother you. And the others too, naturally. It's just that I have to follow the rules. If I don't, they'll have to send somebody else to fill in the gaps. I want to find out, as closely as I can, when Mr Halley—went down to the lake. Whether anyone saw him go.'

He looked around, again.

'As Miss Ross remembers it,' he said, 'she went up to bed a little after one. Perhaps as late as one-thirty. Miss Latham had gone up a few minutes before. Mr Boyd a little earlier. Mr Halley, Mrs Halley, Mr Kemper and Dr Perry were still here, as she recalls it. Is that as you remember it, Mr Boyd?'

'I guess so,' Boyd said. 'Fact is, I went to sleep for a few minutes. Right over there.' He pointed to a chair. 'Something waked me up and I figured I wasn't adding anything to the party and went up to bed. I didn't notice the time. Maybe around one.'

'And went to bed? And turned off your light?'

Boyd appeared puzzled.

'I don't see—' he said. 'But, sure. Been a long

time since I was afraid of the dark.'

'Miss Latham?'

'I guess so,' she said. 'How we can—sit here like this—go over and over and over things that don't matter...'

'And went to bed and turned off your light?'

'Yes. *Yes.*'

'I went up a few minutes after Miss Ross,' Brian Perry said. 'I went to my room, which is on the front—toward the lake—and went to bed and turned off my light. As I was closing my door, I heard someone coming up the stairs and looked back and saw Kemper. I said, "Goodnight again," or something like that.'

Heimrich looked at Kemper, who nodded.

'Way I remember it,' he said. 'I went in and went to bed and turned off my light. What's so important about turning off the lights?'

'Now Mr Kemper,' Heimrich said. 'They're very insistent on all these little details. Nothing important. And you, Mrs Halley—or should I say "Doctor" Halley?' She merely shrugged. 'Stayed up with your husband for a time and left him by the fire and went upstairs.'

'I've told you that several times,' she said.

'And went to bed and to sleep?'

'And—turned out my light. I must say, I share Tom's inability to—'

'Yes,' Heimrich said. 'I realize how trivial it all is, naturally. How—almost unbearable at a time like this. All this—nibbling. However— have you any idea what time you went up, Mrs

73

Halley? Leaving your husband here by the fire?'

'About two.'

Heimrich closed his eyes. He spoke, next, without opening them.

'Did any of you happen to bring a traveling clock along?' he asked. 'An electric clock?'

They looked from one to another. Heimrich opened his eyes.

'I take it not,' he said. 'And after two, none of you saw anything of Mr Halley. Or—heard him go out, say? You, Dr Perry? Since you had a room at the front of the house.'

'No,' Perry said. 'But—perhaps I can help a little. I don't see the importance of this either, captain. But—I didn't go to sleep at once. I seldom do. I was lying so that I looked out a window. I could see the light from the living room—this room—on the snow. It reflected into the room. I heard Dr Halley come up and walk along the hall. Then I dozed. I woke up again, suddenly, an hour or so later. At first I didn't know what had wakened me. Then I realized that it was a change of light in the room—John had turned the light off downstairs. I suppose I had subconsciously been waiting for that, because then I went to sleep.'

'Yes,' Heimrich said. 'One other point. A very small point. Are there electric blankets in most of the guestrooms, Mrs Halley?'

'Electric blankets? I really don't

understand—But, no, captain. We don't use them much in the country. Rural electric service is likely to be erratic. But, I wasn't sure there would be enough blankets and comforters for everybody, so we brought up the one blanket from town.' She turned, quickly, to Lynn. 'My dear,' she said. 'Don't tell me it didn't work?'

'It—' Lynn began, and Heimrich interrupted her.

'It worked quite well,' Heimrich said. 'Very well indeed.' He closed his eyes again. The silence was uneasy. They waited for him to resume. He did not.

'Well,' Boyd said, finally, and his voice was unexpectedly loud after the quiet, 'you've got all the details you want, captain?'

Heimrich opened his very blue eyes.

'All but one,' he said. 'Which of you murdered Mr Halley?'

CHAPTER FIVE

Reaction to Heimrich's statement had been various, and not in all cases what might have been expected. Struthers Boyd had lowered his head into his hands and said, 'Oh, God!' in the tone of a man to whose many tribulations one more, and a ponderous one, had been added. Margaret Halley had stood up and said, in a strange, hard voice, 'You must be out of your mind,' and, when Heimrich merely, slowly, shook his head, had added, 'He killed himself, I tell you. *I tell you he killed himself.*' And then she had looked around at the others, her face white, and her mouth twisted. Then, very abruptly, she had turned and left the room. And Kemper had said, 'Margaret, wait a minute,' and, when she did not, had gone after her. Heimrich merely watched.

'You seem to be quite certain,' Brian Perry had said, in a voice without inflection, and to this Heimrich had nodded. Boyd had got up, said, 'Oh, God!' once more, in a hopeless tone, and had gone out of the room. Audrey Latham had stood up, and she was not white, but flushed. Then the blood drained out of her face and she grasped the arm of a chair and swayed, as if about to fall. Ray Crowley reached her and took her shoulders, but she said, 'No. I'm all right,' and then, to Heimrich, 'I want to talk to you. I've got something to tell you.'

'I thought you might have,' Heimrich said. He looked at Lynn, at Brian Perry. Perry said, 'Yes, I see,' and stood up and Lynn stood too. 'Wants us out of here,' Brian said, unnecessarily, and they went out of there. At the stairs in the entrance hall, Lynn hesitated. 'Come along,' Perry said. 'We'll find something to eat.'

She looked at him. She looked up at him.

'Yes,' he said. 'It's something we can't get

76

away from, Miss Ross. Come on.' He took her arm, gently. He directed her to the door of the dining room. In the dining room, at the sideboard, Struthers Boyd was pouring from a decanter into a glass. He looked at them, and shook his head. He said, 'God, what a mess,' and returned to pouring. Brian Perry and Lynn went on into the breakfast room beyond.

'See what I can do,' Perry said, and went through the door to the kitchen. He came back almost at once. He said, 'She's already fixing sandwiches.' He went to the window and stood looking out of it for a moment. He said, 'Started to snow again. I was afraid it would.' He turned back and pulled a chair around and sat in it, facing Lynn.

'What about the blanket?' he asked. He took off his glasses as she told him. (He looks so different with those glasses off, Lynn thought. Rimless glasses are so—) She finished telling him. She said, 'I don't see what it means.'

'Neither—' Brian began, and stopped suddenly. He said he'd be damned. He looked at Lynn and she shook her head.

'My dear girl,' Brian said. 'Think about it. Use your pretty head.'

'I did something wrong about the blanket,' she said. 'Turned it off instead of on.'

'I told you to *think*,' he said, somewhat sternly.

'Oh,' she said. 'The power went off?'

'Precisely,' Brian said. 'I knew—'

The kitchen door opened. Mrs Speed came in, carrying a plate of sandwiches and a pot of coffee. She set both down on the table, shook her head, sighed deeply and said, 'Dear, oh *dear*!' Then she went back into the kitchen. Brian said, after her and absently, 'Thank you.' He made no move toward the food.

'The power went off,' he said, and talked as much to himself as to Lynn. But, it seemed to hold her attention. He reached out and took her wrist, gently, in a long-fingered hand. 'John was still up. So, he did the inevitable thing. Went to start the generator. He told us there was one, but that it operated manually. Remember?'

'Yes,' Lynn said. 'I remember, doctor.'

'Name's Brian,' Perry said. 'Same as it was last night. That's the way they've figured it. So—' He stopped. 'That's not good enough, is it?' he said. 'I mean, it explains why he was there, but not that he was murdered. Eliminates suicide, probably. But only makes an accident more likely. But this man Heimrich—what do you think of Heimrich, by the way?'

'I don't know,' she said. 'Dogged? Slow and—'

'I thought that,' Brian said. 'Until the last thing he said. Now—I doubt he's slow, my dear. Think that because he's solidly built, probably. Nothing to do with the mind. I wonder—' He turned and reached for the

78

sandwiches. He took one and raised it toward his mouth. He said, 'Oh. Sorry, Lynn. Here,' and held the plate to her. She took a sandwich. 'Know men who would say that proves I was afraid of starvation as a child,' he said. 'You'll have to get used to it. I forget to pass things.'

'Have to—' she said, and did not finish. 'I don't see either. About the power going off, I mean. I suppose he would—I mean Mr Halley would—go out, even on that kind of night, and start the generator? Not wait until morning.'

'My dear child,' Brian Perry said. 'You're in the country. Where do you think the heat comes from? Cold night, the wind rising—we'd have frozen in our beds. Worse. The pipes would have frozen.'

'It isn't heated by electricity,' Lynn said, and then was startled to find that she was blushing. 'I'm stupid,' she said. 'You have to have electricity for an oil burner, don't you?'

'Oil burner,' he said. 'Water. Comes out of a well, my dear. Refrigeration. They may have a Deep Freeze. Probably have. If you've got a generator, you turn it on. John would have gone out, all right. Did go, evidently. But where does the captain get—' He stopped, abruptly. He said, 'Of *course*,' in the tone of one just extricated from his own stupidity. He said, 'We're not very bright, my dear. The power didn't *go* off.'

Lynn took a bite of sandwich. She chewed very slowly and carefully. She swallowed. She said, 'But you just said it did.'

'Didn't *go* off,' he said. 'Was cut off. That's it. Has to be it. You tell Heimrich about your blanket going off. He thinks, "Oh, that explains it. Power failed. Halley went off to turn on the generator. Fell in the lake." But, being a thorough man—they do like to know times, probably, although I doubt whether anybody's breathing down the back of his neck about them—he calls the light company. Says, "When did the power fail in the Lake Carabec area?" And they say, "It didn't fail, captain." And he says, "A-ha!"'

'Somehow,' Lynn said, 'I can't hear him.'

'Words to that effect,' Brian said. 'Probably, actually, he says, "So that's the way it was done."'

Brian got up and poured coffee. He poured two cups, and brought one to Lynn. 'Getting better, aren't I?' he said. He sat down and began to drink coffee. 'I'd like a little cream,' Lynn Ross said, breaking it gently. He laughed, briefly, at himself, and took her cream.

'I suppose it's clear,' Lynn said. 'To Captain Heimrich. Apparently to you.'

'A clear enough theory,' Brian Perry said. He looked at her, appeared to see doubt in her face. 'Trouble is,' he said, 'you don't think. The idea was to get John to go out of the house, down to the lake, so he could be hit over the head and pushed in. Nice, simple plan. But how do you get him to do it? It's no good going to him and saying, "How about taking a little walk? Let's go down and look at the lake." Not on a night like last night. So, you get him to go by putting the lights out. Pulling the main switch, I'd suppose.' He looked at her doubtfully. 'You know what a main switch is?' he asked.

She said she supposed it turned everything off.

'That's it,' he said. 'Somewhere—probably in the basement—there's an electric panel. Fuses and things like that in a box. There's another box—' He paused and looked at her.

'I've always lived in apartments,' she said. 'With superintendents.'

'All right,' he said. 'In this second box, there's a—thing—like a little drawer. It fits tight. If you pull it out, you cut off all the current in the house. What Heimrich's decided—if I'm right, that is—is that somebody pulled it out. Halley's light went out. Halley changed his shoes, and went down to the boathouse to start the generator. Whoever it was, followed him. Probably walked in the tracks Halley had made in the snow. Killed Halley, came back to the house, put the switch back where it belonged, turned off the light in the living room and went to bed. Leaving a choice—suicide or accident. Clear now?'

She thought, as he had told her to do. He

81

watched her, and nodded. She said, 'Wait a minute,' and he waited.

'Whoever it was didn't give Mr Halley time to start the generator?'

'No.'

'Why? I mean—why not let him start it? Put this switch thing back in, but leave the generator running. Then, when Mr Halley was—found—it would have been clear what happened. An accident. The police would—' She stopped. She said, 'Oh. Perhaps it wouldn't have worked with the power on?'

'No,' Brian said. 'You can think, can't you, my dear? And, even if that weren't true—or could be got around—the police would do just what they did do. Find out the power had not gone off. As it was done—if it *was* done this way—it would stay heads or tails, suicide or accident, take your choice. Only—your blanket went off. Something that hadn't been counted on.'

There was rather a long pause. This was, Lynn thought, a very different Brian Perry from the Brian Perry of the night before. There had been a warmth, then. Gentleness. Or, she had thought so.

'You're very detached about this, aren't you?' she said. 'As if it were—an abstract problem. Instead of—wasn't Mr Halley a friend of yours?'

He put his coffee cup down. He lighted a cigarette. He held the package out to her, and

82

she shook her head.

'Cold-blooded, you mean?' he said. 'Yes—I'd known John for several years. We used to see quite a bit of the Halleys. Carla and I. Carla was my wife. We had a small place on the other side of the lake. Near the club. No, I'm not especially cold-blooded.' He reached for his glasses, which he had put on the table. He put the glasses on.

'If I need to explain, there's no point in explaining,' he said. 'But—there's nothing that's made better by not thinking about it, Miss Ross.' He looked at her, thoughtfully. 'All right,' he said, 'the situation is emotional. You, for example, were emotionally shocked. Violence is emotionally shocking. I don't mean you were grieved. I don't know about that—I should think not, greatly. You didn't know John Halley well. You call him "Mister Halley." But—shocked by violence. By the *closeness* of violence. Isn't that true?'

She hesitated; reached toward the package of cigarettes and was handed them. But she did not take a cigarette from the package.

'Perhaps,' she said. 'I suppose you're right.'

'And now?'

'A minute ago,' she said, 'I was annoyed at you. At both of us. For—treating it all like a problem. From—outside.'

'Good,' he said. 'Best thing you can do with your mind, my dear. Use it. Best thing for it. Use.'

'My mind's all right,' she said. She took a cigarette from the package. He watched, politely. 'I'm afraid I haven't a match,' Lynn said. 'I'm sorry,' he said, and held a lighter to the cigarette.

Lynn said, 'Was this therapy?'

He laughed, briefly.

'A very bright child,' he said. 'But—no. Good for you but, as you say, your mind's all right. No. I'm not particularly detached, either. Just want to get things straight because—it may be important. To me.'

'To you?' she said. 'Why to you, Brian?'

'Because John died by drowning,' he said. 'In this particular lake.'

*   *   *

'You waited to be sure everyone was asleep?' Heimrich said. The slim girl in slacks and a sweater sat on the edge of a chair, leaning forward. She sat, now, with her hands pressed against her forehead. She nodded her head.

She had begun almost defiantly; had said, speaking hurriedly, as if the words had long been formed, could no longer be retained. She had said that she and John Halley had loved each other. And then, 'That's why she killed him.'

'She?' Heimrich had said. 'Who, Miss Latham?'

'His wife,' she said. 'Margaret Halley.
84

Doctor Halley. Because he loved me, not her. Haven't you heard her? "It must have been suicide. He was in a depression."' She mimicked the clipped enunciation of Margaret Halley, the level voice. 'Laying the ground work,' Audrey Latham said. 'I thought you realized all the time. I—I thought that's what you meant.'

'Now Miss Latham,' Heimrich said. 'I meant only what I said. That someone— someone in the house now—killed Mr Halley. I don't know who. Yet.'

'I just told you,' Audrey said. Her voice was a little shrill. 'Didn't you hear me?'

'Yes,' Heimrich said. 'I heard you. You accuse Mrs Halley of killing her husband because he was in love with you. Of having laid the ground work, as you say—prepared an explanation in advance—by saying that he was in a depression, and so might kill himself. But, it needs more than that.'

'There is more,' she said. 'I saw her. Coming back upstairs after she had killed him. Oh—I didn't realize it then, of course. That she had finally managed it. Somehow got him to go down to the lake and—pushed him, I suppose. So that he slipped. I don't know all of it.' She stopped suddenly. 'I don't understand about Miss Ross's blanket,' she said. 'I'll admit that.'

Heimrich closed his eyes. He said, 'When was this? That you say you saw Mrs Halley?'

'When I was going back to my room.'

85

Heimrich sighed. 'Suppose,' he said, 'you give it to me in order. You went upstairs a little earlier than the others, except Mr Boyd. You went to your room. And?'

'I waited. We had arranged it, John and I. He was to wait—wait until all the others had gone. Then I was to go down. He—he had something he wanted to tell me. About something he had planned for us.'

'You don't know what?'

'How can I?' she said, and then she put her hands up to her head and sat crouched on the edge of the chair. 'How can I? Ever? Ever in the world?'

Her voice shook. Heimrich waited. He said:

'You waited to be sure everyone was asleep?'

She nodded her head. 'Go on, Miss Latham,' Heimrich said. He closed his eyes to listen. Now and then, as she did go on, he prompted her with questions.

She had gone out of her room, she thought, at about three o'clock—a little before or a little after. The house had been still, yet had talked faintly as houses do—talked in small creakings, in little, inexplicable, cracking sounds. A house is never tired of talking to itself. And she heard the wind outside. It seemed much louder than it had earlier in the night.

She first made sure the others were asleep, or as sure as she could make. Shoeless, carrying slippers—and wearing a robe, now—she went

86

on bare feet, carefully, along the upstairs halls. 'If there's a light, it shows under the doors,' she said. 'The doors have cracks under them. You know?'

Heimrich nodded.

Satisfied that the others were asleep, that she and John Halley would not be interrupted, she had, finally, gone down the back stairs. The stairs came down into a hallway off which the pantry and the big kitchen opened. There had been no one there. She had gone that way so that she could be sure the Speeds were not still around.

'Did you have a flashlight?'

She had not had a flash. But it was not really dark in the house; not once you got used to it. 'There was a—a kind of glow. Coming through the windows. Almost like moonlight.'

Heimrich nodded. Behind the snow clouds there had been a moon the night before. The light of the moon had seemed to seep through the clouds, reflect softly from the fallen snow. He had noticed it, driving back to the Old Stone Inn after he had taken Susan home. The night had been luminous. There had been light enough to seep into rooms through uncurtained windows.

She had left the backstairs area by a door which opened into the central hall. She had gone softly through the hall and, seeing no light from the living room when she neared it, she had assumed those doors closed. But when

87

she did reach the doors, they were open, and the big room was dark—dark except for the red flickering of the dying fire. She had thought, at first, that John Halley was still there, waiting by firelight. But she had seen almost at once that he was not sitting in front of the fire.

She had gone a little way into the room and spoken his name in a whisper, and there had been no response.

'I thought—I don't know what I thought,' she said. 'That I had misunderstood him—must have misunderstood him. Because I knew that if he had said he would wait, he would wait. I was *sure* of that.'

There was, Heimrich thought, sitting with closed eyes, an odd emphasis in the last words. Even now, she was assuring herself of that—of something which, twelve hours or less ago, she had sought with sudden anxiety to assure herself.

She had, she said, thought that perhaps she had misunderstood the place of the meeting—that the arrangement had been that he would come to her room, after it was certain the others were asleep. He might have gone up the main stairway as she, too cautiously, had gone down the back stairs. He might, as she spoke his name so softly in the living room, be puzzledly speaking hers in the room upstairs.

She had started, quickly, back the way she had come.

'Why not the front stairs?' Heimrich asked.

88

'I don't know,' she said. 'I just went back the way I had come down.'

At the rear of the central hall, under the main staircase, near the door from the kitchen, were stairs leading down to the cellar. They were not closed off by a door; there was a rail across the top of the flight, and it was closed and latched into place. As she passed these stairs she had heard sounds from the basement.

'Sounds?' Heimrich asked. 'What sort of sounds, Miss Latham?'

'I thought, somebody moving,' she said. 'I thought, for a moment, John's gone down there to do something.'

She had stopped and listened. As she listened, and peered down into the darkness, she had become less sure of the nature of the sounds she had heard. It was possible, she thought, that she had merely heard 'house sounds'—or the furnace popping as it cooled a little. Or, perhaps, some animal, which had gone into the basement for warmth. Nevertheless, she had gone part way down the stairs and, again, she had whispered John Halley's name. There had been no answer from the darkness below.

She had gone back up a few steps, until she could reach a light switch. She had turned the light on. 'A very bright light,' she said. 'Hanging down from a cord.'

Heimrich opened his eyes, then.

'The light went on?' he asked her.

'Why,' she said, 'of course. Why wouldn't it?'

'No reason,' Heimrich said. 'I take it you saw no one?'

She had not. She could not see all of the basement—she had gone no farther, even with the light on, than half way down the flight. The light left many parts of the big basement in dense shadow. But, she had seen no one. Nor had she, again, heard the sounds. It had been very quiet among the shadows. She had said, once more, 'John?' and again got no answer. She had then gone back up the basement stairs.

'Did you turn the light off?'

'I don't remember,' she said. 'I suppose I did.'

Then she had gone up the back stairs, returning to the second floor. She had gone up them slowly, cautiously, still in her bare feet. She had groped her way along the upper hall, had come to its juncture with the hall which ran from front to rear of the house, and started into it. There was more light there. From where she stood, she could see the top of the main stairs.

'Mrs Halley was coming up them,' she said. 'I—I didn't want her to see me. I drew back.'

But not so far back that she could not still, from the relative darkness, watch Margaret Halley.

'She was carrying something. I couldn't see what. Something in her right hand. She kept her left hand on the stair rail.'

90

When she reached the top of the stairs, Margaret Halley had gone through the hall toward the front of the house, and then to her left and out of sight in the hall at right angles to the central hall. 'The Halleys' bedrooms open off it,' Audrey Latham said. Telling the story seemed to have steadied her; she still sat on the edge of her chair, and leaned a little forward, but she seemed less tense. 'Her room's at the end of that hall,' Audrey said. 'A corner room.'

'You couldn't see what she was carrying?'

'I said I couldn't. Something you could carry in one hand.'

'Did she see you?'

'I don't know.' Her eyes went blank for an instant. 'I don't think so.'

When Mrs Halley had gone out of sight, and Audrey had waited until she could no longer hear her footsteps, Audrey had gone on along the hall to her own room; had entered it and, once more, said, 'John?' And once more she had not been answered. She had turned on the light. The room was empty.

'And then?'

'I went to bed. I couldn't understand what had happened but—I supposed it was something about Margaret's being up, which—which had kept John from waiting for me. I remember I thought, it will be all right in the morning. There'll be another time. And—after a while I went to sleep.' She put her head in her hands again. '*Went to sleep!*' she said.

'Just went to sleep. And she—*she was coming back after she'd killed John!*'

'Now Miss Latham,' Heimrich said. 'What you tell us doesn't prove that. You see that, naturally.'

'What?' she said. She looked hard at Heimrich; did not see what, apparently, she had hoped to see. 'It's you who *don't* see,' she said. '*Won't* see. Why? Because she's well known? Because the Halleys have a lot of money? Or—John had a lot of money? Is there something—sacred about "Doctor" Halley?' Her tone put quotation marks around the word Doctor.

'Now Miss Latham,' Heimrich said. 'What was Mrs Halley wearing when you saw her?'

'Something dark,' Audrey said. 'A dark coat.'

'Or, a dark robe?'

'Look,' the blond girl said, 'she had to go out in the snow to kill him. Down to the lake. She'd wear a coat, wouldn't she?'

'What you saw,' Heimrich said. 'Not what you think it must have been. Could it have been a dark robe?'

She hesitated. Finally she said she supposed so.

'But,' she said, 'it must have been a coat. You're trying to protect her.'

Heimrich opened his eyes.

'Did she see you? *Could* she have seen you, Miss Latham?'

'I don't think so.'

'But—whoever was in the basement. If anyone was. Whoever it was could have seen you, naturally. When you were standing on the stairs?'

She supposed so. But she did not, now, think there had been anybody in the basement.

'What are you going to do?' she demanded.

Heimrich sighed.

'Find out who killed Mr Halley,' he said. 'Is there anything else you want to tell us?'

'About—' she began, and suddenly stood up. 'What's the use?' she said. 'I'm wasting time, aren't I? You're so high and mighty—so sure—you find out the rest.'

And, very abruptly, she left the room.

'Upset,' Heimrich said. 'Natural she should be, of course. For one reason or another. I suppose the electric panel is in the basement, Charlie?'

'Suppose so,' Forniss said, and looked at Ray Crowley, who went to find out. It took him only a few minutes. He returned and said, 'Yes, it is.'

'We'll have to print it, I suppose,' Heimrich said. 'If we don't, somebody'll ask us why we didn't. No point in having to say, "Because we didn't want to waste time," is there?'

'Nope,' Forniss said, and went out to the car for what he needed, and to the basement, to waste the approved amount of time. He used a flash to augment the faint light from a dim,

93

dangling bulb.

The telephone rang while Forniss wasted time. At a nod from Heimrich, Trooper Crowley answered it. He came back to say that Dr Kramer was on the wire, and had news. Heimrich went into the hall, and talked to the county pathologist. He learned that examination of the viscera of John Halley disclosed that, shortly before his death, he had ingested a massive overdose of a barbiturate—probably Nembutal. The total dose might prove to have been as much as two and a half grams, which would have proved fatal, failing immediate and drastic treatment.

It had not proved fatal, because Mr Halley had drowned first.

'Have a good time,' Dr Kramer said pleasantly, and hung up.

CHAPTER SIX

Struthers Boyd stood in the doorway of the breakfast room. He had a drink in his hand; it was not, Lynn found herself thinking, the drink he had been pouring when they passed him at the sideboard. He stood in the doorway and looked most sad, his face drooping. Although Lynn was not young enough to think him aged, he did seem appreciably older than he had the night before. Joviality had seeped out of him; he was no longer hearty.

'Old John,' Boyd said. 'Good old John. Oh, God! Best friend a man ever had. Remember in our senior year—' The memory appeared to overcome him.

'Come on in,' Brian Perry said. 'Have some coffee.' Perry felt the pot. 'Still pretty hot,' he said.

Boyd came in, carrying his glass. He shook his head gloomily at the coffee pot.

'Just make things clearer,' he said. 'This is better.' He put the glass down on the table and patted it. 'Best friend a man ever had.' He seemed to be puzzled by his own words. 'John, I mean,' he said. 'Do anything for you. What I mean, anything. Remember in our junior year—'

'Here, Struthers,' Perry said, and poured coffee into a cup. 'You'd better, really.'

'You're the doctor,' Boyd said. He sat. He picked the coffee cup up and looked at its contents and put it down. He picked his glass up. He drank from it.

'What's he mean, somebody murdered old John?' Boyd asked. 'You know what he means? *You* know what he means?' He addressed the question first to Lynn, then to Brian Perry.

'What he said, I suppose,' Brian said. 'Somebody wanted John dead. Hit him on the head. Knocked him into the lake.'

'Nobody would do a thing like that,' Boyd

said. 'Not to old John. You know what he did?'

They shook their heads.

'In which year?' Brian asked, gravely.

'Which year?' Boyd said. 'Don't know what you mean by that, fella.'

'I'm sorry,' Brian Perry said. 'I thought you were talking about college, Struth.'

'Classmates,' Boyd said. 'I tell you that? Class of 'twenty-two.' He looked at Lynn and shook his head. 'Before you were born,' he said. 'Getting along, poor old John was. But you wouldn't have known it. That right, Brian? Wouldn't have known it, would you?' He drank further from his glass. 'Girls didn't know it either,' he said. 'Like Grace says—' He stopped. 'My wife,' he said, to Lynn. 'In Florida. Did I tell you what John did?'

'No,' Lynn said. 'I don't think you did, Mr Boyd.'

'I got hold of this—thing,' Boyd said. 'Know what I mean?'

The question was presumed rhetorical.

'Plastic thing,' Boyd said. 'Can't tell you any more than that. See why I can't, don't you?'

Lynn looked at Brian Perry. Her expression said that this, added to the rest, was quite definitely too much. Her expression accurately reflected her thought. But she was surprised to see that Brian Perry was leaning a little forward, watching with an odd intentness the big man with the sagging face; listening intently to the big man's wandering words.

'A secret thing,' Perry said. 'Sure, we understand, Struth. Something you've picked up the patent on? Are going to manufacture?'

'That's it,' Boyd said. 'Going to revolutionize—can't tell you what it's going to revolutionize, can I?'

'No,' Perry said, 'you can't. What did John do?'

'What I said,' Boyd told him. 'I just told you, didn't I?'

Brian merely shook his head. His eyes, behind the rimless glasses, were unreadable.

'Put up the money,' Boyd said. 'All I've got's tied up in this and that. You know how things are?'

'Sure,' Brian said.

'Thought at first I'd have to let it go. Then I thought—why not let old John in on it? Remembered how in our sophomore year—' He shook his head, seemingly overcome by remembrance. 'Put it up to John. Know what he did?'

'Came through,' Perry said. 'That's what he did, wasn't it?'

'Knew I'd told you,' Boyd said. 'Went to him and put the cards on the table. Said, "Here's the picture, John." Told him what I needed to swing it. How much he'd be cut in for. Know what he said?' This was entirely rhetorical; no answer was invited. 'Said, "We'll worry about that when we come to it, Struth, old man." Meant the cut, you understand. Sat down and wrote me a check. Just like that. That's the kind of man old John was. Best friend a man ever—'

He shook his head; he finished his glass.

'Don't want to talk about it,' he said. 'Never had anything hit me so hard, Brian.' He stood up. 'Nobody knew John better'n I did. You can see why, can't you? Why'd anybody kill a man like old John?'

He did not wait for an answer. He shook his head. Holding his glass, he turned and walked out of the room.

'Well,' Lynn said, without approval, when Boyd was, presumably, out of earshot. 'What was that all about?'

She waited for an answer. She looked at Brian Perry, who was looking at the door through which Boyd had gone; whose air of intentness remained. It was some seconds before he turned toward her, and took his glasses off. His eyes were still a little narrowed.

'I was wondering,' he said. 'I was wondering very much, my dear. Boyd used to spend a good deal of time at the club. Still does, for all I know. I'm speaking of the time Carla and I lived on the lake. He had a reputation—rather an outstanding reputation. Not as a man who drank a great deal. But—as a man who never showed he'd been drinking at all.'

'Well,' Lynn said, 'he seems to have changed.'

'Yes,' Brian agreed. 'He does seem to have

98

changed. I wonder why, Lynn.'

She didn't know what he meant. She said so. She added that, after all, Struthers Boyd had dozed off toward the end of the party.

'Without, up to then, showing any sign he'd been drinking,' Brian said. 'Did you notice that? And—he had been. More than the rest of us. As for going to sleep—he was tired when he arrived. Under strain. Didn't you notice that?'

'No,' she said.

'Easy enough to tell,' Perry said. 'If you know what to look for, I suppose. He drank to relax his nerves. And did. But, without getting drunk, my dear. And now today—' He shrugged. 'Also, you notice he didn't slur his words? "Revolutionize" can trip the tongue.'

'You mean he was pretending?'

'I thought so. Exaggerating, at any rate.'

'He's very—sunk,' Lynn said. 'At Mr Halley's death. He seems to have been devoted to Mr Halley. Mightn't that—I mean his psychological condition—make him more susceptible?'

'Possibly,' Brian Perry said. 'Oh, quite possibly. A willingness to seek—and accept— the softening of impressions, the comfortable blur. Only—'

She waited.

'Well,' he said, 'I've always thought that Boyd, under that hail-classmate-well-met manner of his was about as shrewd and competent as they come. And—about as unsentimental as they come. And—it never occurred to me until just now that he and John Halley were particularly devoted friends.'

He continued to look at her, although now his eyes were no longer narrowed.

'In fact,' he said, 'I hadn't supposed that John Halley had any. Among men, at any rate. Not that one would call devoted.'

*　　　*　　　*

Heimrich waited until Forniss had reported that, on the fuse box and in its vicinity, he had found nothing to report. The narrow loop of wire by which the main fuse could be pulled from its socket would, at best, have taken prints too partial for usefulness. Forniss had found not even partial prints. If it had been handled, it had been wiped afterward.

'Naturally,' Heimrich said, and told Sergeant Forniss of the report of the county pathologist. Forniss said, 'Ouch!'

'Yes, Charlie,' Heimrich said. 'It's disconcerting, isn't it? I may have gone out on a limb. He may have taken a lethal dose of whatever it was and sat by the fire waiting for it to work. Might take as much as an hour to work, you know. While he's waiting, the lights go out. Conscientious man, even to the end, or near it. I wonder if he was, Charlie?'

Forniss could merely shrug heavy shoulders.

'Yes,' Heimrich said, 'that's one of the
100

problems, isn't it? We don't know much about him—except he was fifty-five or so, had a good deal of money, never had to work for a living. Be pleasant not to have to work for a living, wouldn't it?'

'Sure,' Forniss said. 'In a boring sort of way.'

'Now Charlie,' Heimrich said. 'On New Year's Day, anyway. I had a date.' He paused to consider this. The fact surprised him. 'With Mrs Faye,' he said. 'To drink eggnog. A noxious drink, ordinarily. Still—' He looked at his watch. It was almost three. He would have to use the telephone; he should have done so before now.

'Suppose,' Heimrich said, 'we say he was a conscientious man. Man who, even when he was waiting to die, keeps his house going. Especially when it was full of guests. Seem likely, Charlie?'

'Not very,' Forniss said. 'But—sure, it could be.'

'Say it is,' Heimrich said. 'We can't prove it wasn't, can we? He goes down to the boathouse, planning to start the generator. But, just before he gets there, the stuff hits him. He gets dizzy, confused, ataxia sets in. In other words, he becomes likely to fall into anything. He falls into the lake. Drowns before the Nembutal kills him. Attempted suicide; actual death by accident. And, we're on a limb.'

'Nope,' Charlie said. 'Why did the lights go

101

out?'

'Now Charlie,' Heimrich said. 'I'm talking about proof—not what we think. This caretaker's clock may have been fast for days, and he never noticed it. Hasn't much need to know the exact time, probably. Miss Ross may have done something to the blanket, as she first thought she did. She couldn't very well deny she had thought that, could she? And—if we could prove it, what would we have? Malicious mischief. You'll have to admit it's disconcerting, Charlie.'

'Somebody in the cellar,' Forniss said. 'And Mrs Halley going downstairs and sneaking back up.'

'Coming back up,' Heimrich said. 'If anybody was sneaking it was our little Audrey. If there was anything in the cellar, it was a rat. Maybe a squirrel. Places like this get full of squirrels in the winter. When we ask her, Mrs Speed will tell us there were nut shells all over the place when she came to clean up for the party.'

'All right,' Forniss said. 'We tell them we're sorry. Pack up and go home.'

'Now Charlie,' Heimrich said. He got up and walked to a window and looked out. Snow was falling heavily again—more heavily, he thought, than at any time before. And a wind was driving it. A north-east wind, now. 'We'd need snowshoes,' Heimrich said. 'Or skis. I wonder—'

He did not say what he wondered. Instead he crossed the room and went out to the telephone in the hall. To the operator, when she answered, he said, 'Weather, please,' and waited.

'—for New York City and vicinity,' a precise, slightly metallic, voice said. 'Three P.M. temperature twenty-seven degrees; barometer twenty-nine point seven five and falling. Moderate to heavy snow this afternoon and tonight, probably continuing into tomorrow. Maximum accumulation six to nine inches. Increasing northeast winds, becoming fresh to strong late this afternoon and continuing strong tonight. Forecast for New York City and vicinity. Three P.M. temperature—'

Heimrich hung up. He dialed the operator again. He gave a number in the Town of Van Brunt, heard the ringing signal, said, 'Mrs Faye?'

'This is Susan,' she said.

'You're all right?' he said. 'I mean—'

'Snug as a bug,' she said. 'I gather you're not coming around?'

He told her why he was not coming around. He swallowed. He said, 'I wonder whether some evening during the week—' There was great doubt in his tone. He realized he was speaking softly, presumably so that Sergeant Forniss would not overhear him. He felt somewhat embarrassed. 'Almost any evening,'

103

Susan Faye said. He felt fine. Even if murder did seem to be taking on the paler hue of malicious mischief. He made a call to the headquarters of Troop K, at Hawthorne. There was a special advisory that the snow in northern Westchester might reach the depth of a foot or more. Cars were stalling everywhere—and sliding into one another, and into ditches. What could be done would of course be done. He called New York, and the headquarters of Homicide West. He talked to Sergeant Stein, on duty. Sergeant Stein took notes—notes of names. He would get things in the works.

'Snowing here,' Stein said. 'Snowing where you are?'

'Yes,' Heimrich said, mildly, and hung up and went back into the living room.

'Get her all right?' Forniss said.

'Yes,' Heimrich said. 'We'll maybe get a foot of snow.'

It was growing dark in the room; already the short afternoon was ebbing. He turned on several of the lamps.

'You want Mrs Halley?' Forniss said.

'I suppose so,' Heimrich said. 'It's a gloomy day, isn't it. Yes, I suppose we'd better—' He broke off. 'No,' he said. 'Not yet. We'll work around the edges, Charlie. Let's see what the other—'

He was interrupted. Ray Crowley came in, carrying a tray. There were sandwiches on the

104

tray and a pot of coffee.

'Compliments of Lucy Speed,' Crowley told them. 'Said, "Those poor men. Even if they are policemen" and, "Here, Ray, take them these." Great old girl for feeding people. Any time I stop by the club—' He did not finish.

They ate, discovering that they were hungry.

'What are they doing, Ray?' Heimrich asked, with the first sandwich finished.

'The tall girl,' Ray said, 'Miss Ross. And the doctor. They're in the breakfast room. Talking. Mr Boyd's in the dining room. He's drinking. I don't know about the rest. Want I should find out?'

'No,' Heimrich said. 'They won't go anywhere. Not in this.'

Crowley went to a window. He said it sure was snowing.

'What do you know about these people, Ray?' Heimrich asked him.

'Not an awful lot,' Crowley said. 'All very law-abiding. Mr Halley spends—used to spend—a good deal of time at the club, I understand. Played a lot of golf. Mr Boyd too, but only on weekends. I just knew who they were, to look at. Boyd's a promoter of some sort, as I get it. Whatever that means, exactly. The Halleys stay here most of the summer. She goes back and forth to town more than he does. Dr Perry and his wife had a house on the lake—other end. They rented it oh—three or four summers. Before she died. He didn't come

105

back after that. Not that I ever heard of, any way. See why he wouldn't want to, after what happened.'

'Happened, Ray? What happened?'

'Mrs Perry was drowned,' Crowley said. 'Didn't you know about that? Summer before last, it was.'

Heimrich was very patient. He said, 'No, Ray. Nobody told me.'

Ray Crowley flushed.

'Water skiing,' Crowley said. 'Hit something—log or something. Sort of thing that happens all the time. Only—she apparently hit her head on something else. A rock, I guess. Didn't find her until the next day. Not that they didn't—'

He stopped, very abruptly.

'I just remembered,' he said. 'Mr Halley was towing her. With the little speed boat he used to have.' He looked at Heimrich, and was very red. 'Hell,' he said. 'I'm not much of a cop, I guess.'

'Well, Ray,' Heimrich said. 'You did remember. So it's all right, Ray. But, I think we might talk to Dr Perry about—'

All the lights in the room went out.

Forniss was on his feet, instantly; he was running—into the hall, along it, his feet fast and heavy on the bare flooring. The house echoed with his running. They could hear him on the cellar stairs. They waited in the dim room, and heard Forniss coming back. He did not hurry, now; it was clear he came alone. He came into the room, and as he did so the house seemed suddenly to come to life behind him. There were voices, the sound of feet.

'Nope,' Forniss said. 'Not this time. This time it's the real thing.'

'Try the telephone, Charlie,' Heimrich said.

Forniss went to the telephone, lifted the receiver and listened. He dialed, and asked for a Mount Kisco number. He listened again, and hung up. He came back. He said the phone was all right.

'Funny thing,' he said. 'It usually is. You'd think if one went the other would. The Company's line's busy.'

'Naturally,' Heimrich said. 'Half the county's calling in by now.'

When the electricity dies, a country house dies. This is not so true of houses in cities and in towns, or of such remote houses as live in other days—which electricity has never brought to life. Such houses are more sturdy; pull thick walls around themselves and peer out of small windows. Fireplaces warm them, and stoves for wood and coal; oil lamps give enough yellow light for their quiet lives. The Halley house might once have been such a house, but that had been long ago. Now, like all its neighbors, it dangled at the end of wires.

Almost at once, when the power failed, the house began to take on the chill of death. This was, at first, more imaginary than real. At first there was only a murky darkness, not yet complete. But darkness is colder than light; there is a chill to the spirit in darkness. And such light as remained would soon fade.

But those in the house, when the power failed, began to stir—to hurry this way and that. There was, instantly, a kind of nervous anxiety permeating the house. The movement was not, in all cases and at first, to any evident purpose. There was the sound of feet on stairs and Audrey Latham—who had changed to a woolen dress—came into the room and said, 'Something's happened to the lights. What's happened to the lights?' Tom Kemper came, in slacks and sweater, and told everyone that this was a hell of a note, and now what? Abner Speed came in from the kitchen with a flashlight, looked at the fireplace and shook his head, and went glumly away again. They could hear his feet on the cellar stairs. Mrs Speed came in carrying a candle in either hand, and there was a small flickering light in the room— light which seemed only to accentuate the darkness.

'I'll bring some more,' Mrs Speed said and sighed deeply. 'It's a terrible thing,' she said, and started out.

'And flashlights,' Heimrich said. 'Bring flashlights, Mrs Speed.'

'Like as not they're dead,' she said. 'Mostly they are.' She sighed again, and went out through the door at the rear of the living room.

Speed came back up the cellar stairs, his footsteps slow and heavy. He came into the living room, carrying wood. He piled it on the hearth and stood up and started out. He stopped, and looked around at them. 'Kindling,' he said.

'Mr Speed,' Heimrich said. 'Can you start the generator?'

'Me?' Speed said and stopped, apparently considering. 'Guess not,' he said. 'Never have. Don't work here regular. Remember that.' He started out into the hall; stopped and said, "Scuse *me*,' in the tone of one who has been bumped into. He had not; he had stopped before colliding with Struthers Boyd, unexpectedly dressed in a heavy windbreak, and wearing a cap with ear protectors. Boyd appeared to be entirely sober.

'Came for the key,' Boyd said. 'Poor old John must have had it on him.'

'Key?' Heimrich said. He regarded Boyd. 'Oh,' he said. 'You mean to the boathouse?'

'Well,' Boyd said, 'we don't want to sit here and freeze, do we? Won't bring poor old John back.' He paused, a little as if he had tripped over his last words. 'Best friend a man ever had,' he said. 'All the same—'

'You know how to get the generator going?' Heimrich asked him.

'Nothing to it,' Boyd said. 'Got one at my place. Press a button and there you are. Unless the battery's down. Or nobody's kept it from

109

freezing up. Or you're out of gas. Just give me the key.'

Heimrich carried a candle to a table in the corner of the room. He picked a key chain from among the few objects John Halley had carried when he died. One of the keys was, obviously, to a padlock. Boyd took the keys and started out. 'Better go with him, Charlie,' Heimrich said. 'Lend a hand. Take a flash.'

'Got to get—' Boyd began. '*Ex*cuse me,' Abner Speed said, blocking his progress, standing with arms full of kindling. 'A shovel,' Boyd said. 'Dig our way in.'

They got a shovel from the basement. Forniss and Boyd plodded through the deepening snow. The tracks to the lake, raggedly sharp two hours before, were now barely visible. They crossed the road and went down the slope toward the lake. Snow had drifted in front of the boathouse door, which was on the lee. They shoveled. In time they got the door open.

The flashlight, which Sergeant Forniss had got from the police car, threw strong, hard light into the low building. There was a catwalk around three sides of a rectangle of dark water. Near the door, where there was just room for it, was a squat mechanism covered with canvas. Working together, they stripped the canvas off. There was nothing in Boyd's efficient movements to show that he had been drinking.

'Starter button ought to be about—' Boyd

110

said, looking. 'Yes. All we've got to do now—'
He pressed the button. There was a grinding
sound—nothing else. He took his finger off the
button; put it back on and pressed hard, his big
finger bending under the strain. With the same
result. 'You try it,' Boyd said, and Forniss did,
and held the button down, and got noise only.

'Could be there's no gas,' Boyd said. 'But I'd
have thought—throw the light over this way.'
Forniss threw the light over that way. 'No,'
Boyd said. 'Not shut off. Must be that—' He
squatted by the generator. He swore, and stood
up again.

'Distributor rotor's out,' he said. 'No
wonder we didn't get anywhere. Now what
the—' He stopped. 'Those damned kids,' he
said. 'That's what it is. Old John outsmarted
them. See what I mean?'

'Nope,' Forniss said, 'I don't know that I do,
Mr Boyd. You mean—kids stole the rotor?'

'Doubt it,' Boyd said. 'More likely John
took it out. Some of those kids are devils. John
was a jump ahead of them.' He paused again.
'And, looks like, of us.'

Forniss waited.

'A bunch of kids around here,' Boyd said.
'Like a dog pack. Some of them will do
anything—Halloween, or just when they find a
place shut up. Tear down the mailboxes. *And*
fences. Mess up anything they can get to.
Couple or three years ago, they got to my
generator and started it up. Went away leaving

111

it running—and laughing like hell, I wouldn't wonder. Would have burned it out, except the gas ran out first. See what I mean now?'

'Yes,' Forniss said. 'I see now.'

'John took the rotor out,' Boyd said. 'Hid it somewhere. Foxed the kids.'

Forniss threw his light around the boathouse but without hope.

'Not a chance,' Boyd said. 'He'd have taken it up to the house. They're monkeys. Find anything he hid here. Bring it down with him when he needed to start the generator up. Snap it on again. Probably had it with him when—' He did not finish. He looked at Forniss. 'Probably had it in his hand,' he said. 'When he went into the lake. Dropped it as he went in. Maybe, flailing around to catch himself, threw it. See what I mean?'

Forniss did. The picture was quite clear. It was, indeed, almost as if Struthers Boyd had seen it happen.

On the way back to the house, through thickly falling snow, with darkness now heavy about them, Sergeant Forniss walked behind Boyd, throwing the light beam in front of them to guide the way.

* * *

They had all come to the living room, as if the flickering candles drew them in the lightless house. Abner Speed had got a fire going in the living room fireplace; it made a great crackling. Flames from the kindling leaped joyfully around the larger logs—and little heat was given off. That would come later; the hottest fire is an old fire. A young fire is merely flirtatious. Speed had gone into the dining room and built another fire there and, with that done, he had gone down into the basement and could be heard moving things. Speed, Heimrich thought, appeared to have little confidence in the generator in the boathouse.

Brian Perry and Lynn Ross had come into the living room together, presumably from the breakfast room. 'Somebody started the generator?' Perry asked, and Heimrich said that he hoped so—that Mr Boyd and the sergeant were trying. 'Boyd?' Brian repeated, in apparent surprise, and then looked at Lynn. Heimrich could not, in the dimness, see enough to interpret the wordless exchange, if there was an exchange to interpret. Tom Kemper came down the stairs rapidly, and, in the living room, spoke rather loudly, as if heartiness would dispel gloom. He, also, enquired about the generator. 'I hope so,' Heimrich said again, although he was beginning not to. Margaret Halley came down the stairs more slowly. She was a slender figure, in a dark woolen dress which had been planned for the accenting brightness of jewelry and was somber without it. Her beautifully articulated face showed strain as she bent toward a candle to light a cigarette. And she said nothing; her attitude was a comment. Audrey Latham came last, wearing slacks and sweater as before. She looked at Heimrich. She said, 'Oh. I thought you'd gone.' She did not seem to expect an answer. She shivered. She said, 'It's cold in here.' But it was not yet really cold.

Mrs Speed returned, this time with several candles. She said, 'Where do you want I should put them, Mrs Halley?' and Margaret Halley, standing near one of the burning candles—still standing so that light from below accentuated the modelling of her face—said first, 'What, Mrs Speed?' as if her mind had been far away, and then, 'Oh. Anywhere.' Mrs Speed, shaking her head, began to light candles, let them drip into ash trays, secure them in the soft wax. The room became just perceptibly brighter.

'Aren't there some old lamps in the cellar?' Tom Kemper said. 'I'm pretty sure I saw some once. Kerosene lamps?'

'I don't know, Tom,' Margaret Halley said, in a voice without expression. 'There may be. I don't know.'

Heimrich moved to a window and looked out it. A light was coming up from the lake; he could make out the two men. He went out of the living room and to the door to meet them, and Forniss said, 'No soap,' and told him why. He went back into the living room and said that something seemed to be wrong with the generator.

They were scattered through the living room, as the flickering candles were scattered. Audrey Latham stood close to the fire; Margaret was sitting in a chair not far from it, and Tom Kemper stood near Audrey. The fire was smoking a little, and the air was becoming faintly acrid with the smoke. Brian Perry and Lynn Ross stood side by side at a window; he held the curtains back with one hand, and they were looking out at the snow. But outside there was only a gray blur to look at. Forniss and Struthers Boyd came into the room.

Abner Speed came along the hall. He carried a lighted oil heater in either hand and the fumes from the heaters merged, unamiably, with the smoke from the fireplace. 'Water pressure's low,' Speed said. 'Better not flush.'

'Oh, my God,' Audrey said. 'Oh, my *God*!'

Speed looked in at her. He shook his head. He went up the stairs toward the second floor, carrying the oil burners.

'Why won't the generator work?' Brian Perry asked. His voice did not reveal strain.

'A part's missing,' Heimrich said. 'Apparently Mr Halley took it out.' He turned to Margaret Halley. 'You didn't know of this—arrangement?' he said. 'To keep boys from starting it up?'

She shook her head. 'I left things like that to him,' she said, in the same expressionless voice, and then, '*Captain*.'

Heimrich waited a moment. He said, 'Yes?'

115

'You can't keep everyone here,' she said. 'Not—with things like this. You must realize that. There'll be no heat. No water.'

'Now Mrs Halley,' Heimrich said. 'How would anyone get away? Until the roads are plowed again?'

'That's right, Margaret,' Kemper said. His voice seemed oddly cheerful. (The gravity has slipped off, Lynn thought—and found that she turned to Brian Perry, looked up at him. He seemed to know why; he nodded his head and smiled, faintly. But his eyes, behind the glasses, were unreadable. I'm all alone here, Lynn thought. I don't belong here. This hasn't anything to do with me.)

'Have to make the best of things,' Boyd said. 'No way out of that. That right, captain?'

'Make the best of murder,' Audrey said, and her voice was shrill, just under control. 'Keep stiff—'

'Be quiet,' Margaret Halley said. 'At least be quiet.' And then she said, 'There was no murder. I tell you, there was no murder.'

Silence greeted that. The fire crackled in the silence. But, Heimrich thought, it was a nervous silence. In it, the heavy footsteps of Abner Speed, coming downstairs again, echoed. Speed came to the door.

'Got the gas stove going in the kitchen,' he said. 'Shouldn't wonder if we use up the gas, though. Not a lot of kerosene, either.' He paused. No one said anything. 'Storm like this

116

can last a couple of days,' he said. 'Knew one lasted three days. Well, bring up some more wood, anyway.'

He went.

'There,' Tom Kemper said, 'is our ray of sunshine. Margaret?'

She said, 'Yes, Tom.'

'Suppose I make everybody a drink?'

'If you want to,' she said. She seemed, with an effort, to rouse herself. 'Of course,' she said. 'It will be good for everyone. You, captain?'

'Not now,' Heimrich said. 'Dr Perry?' Perry looked at him. 'A couple of points,' Heimrich said. 'If you don't mind.'

He was told to shoot.

'In the other room,' Heimrich said. 'There's a fire in there, too.'

He led the way. Perry looked after him a moment. He looked down at Lynn, and, just perceptibly, shrugged his shoulders. He followed Heimrich.

In the dining room, the fire was smouldering. Heimrich put a foot against it and pushed. Flames licked up around the logs.

'Usually works,' Heimrich said. 'Doctor, why did you come here?'

There were only two candles in the square dining room. The revived flames gave a flickering, reddish light. The light flickered on Brian Perry's glasses.

'That's a very odd question, captain,' Perry said. 'What do you mean?'

Heimrich said nothing.

'Obviously,' Perry said, 'because I was invited. Had no other engagement. Thought it might be a pleasant—a different—way to spend a holiday weekend.' He looked at Heimrich from behind the glasses and in the uncertain light Heimrich could not see his eyes. Eyes are revealing—which was one reason Heimrich so often kept his closed. 'Did you think there was something else?'

'I didn't know, doctor,' Heimrich said. 'That was why I asked, naturally. Not professionally, then? As a psychiatrist?'

'No.'

'Although Mr Halley had been in a—a condition which made his suicide likely?'

'I don't know that he had,' Perry said. 'He wasn't my patient, captain.' But then he hesitated; he took off his glasses. 'I take it we're both fencing,' he said.

'Now doctor,' Heimrich said. 'I'm merely trying to get the picture, as they say.'

'Then,' Perry said, 'you should ask Dr Halley why she invited me. That's more to the point, isn't it?'

'In time,' Heimrich said. 'If it seems important. If you don't know?'

Perry turned and looked at the fire. He pushed a log with his foot. He said, 'All right. I suppose professional reticence is a little out of place. You still think Halley was murdered? Tricked into going down to the lake?'

118

'Yes,' Heimrich said.

Perry pulled a chair close to the fire. He sat in it.

'Very well,' he said. 'It wasn't explicit. But Margaret wanted me to look John over. If he was willing, of course. Get a second opinion. As she told you, she thought he was in a psychosis. Felt, properly, that she was too close to him—too involved—to function altogether as a physician.'

'Did you look him over?'

'No. I planned to talk to him today. If he wanted to talk.'

'Last night. Did you pay particular attention to him? Reach some sort of tentative conclusion?'

Perry hesitated a moment. He took time to take a package of cigarettes from his pocket; to extract one and hold it ready for lighting. Then he said, 'No, captain. It isn't that simple.' Then he lighted the cigarette. 'Dr Halley is competent,' he said. 'It isn't likely she would be wrong.' Then he held the cigarette package out to Heimrich. Heimrich took a cigarette.

'Doctor,' Heimrich said, 'how long had Mr Halley been—ill? I'm supposing his wife was right.'

'About eighteen months,' Perry said. 'Since summer before last. Since he—' Perry stopped abruptly. He threw his freshly lighted cigarette into the fire. 'Well,' he said. 'I suppose you know. And that that's what this is really about.'

'The summer your wife died,' Heimrich said. 'Yes. I was coming to that, doctor. She was water skiing. Mr Halley was pulling her in a motorboat. She ran into something, lost her balance and—'

'And Halley killed her,' Brian Perry said, and his voice suddenly was harsh. 'Her name was Carla. She would have been twenty-six that September. She was wearing a white bathing suit and she was very brown from being in the sun. And Halley killed her.' Abruptly, he took a fresh cigarette from the pack. The flare of the lighter showed his face. The lines of his face were bitter.

'Killed her?' Heimrich said. 'Why do you put it that way, doctor? She lost her balance, in falling struck her head on a rock. You mean—he shouldn't have been in that part of the lake? Or—what *do* you mean, doctor?'

'It's very simple,' Perry said. 'I thought I had been clear. He killed her. Oh—it festered in his mind afterward. I don't doubt that. He was left with a feeling of guilt. And Carla—Carla was left dead—' He stopped, abruptly and rubbed the palm of one hand hard across his forehead. 'All right,' he said. 'There you have it. And—he died in somewhat the same way, didn't he? Hit on the head. Drowned. Well?'

'No,' Heimrich said, 'you haven't been clear. It's not really clear what you're talking about, doctor.'

120

Brian Perry did not answer immediately. He took his glasses off and held them in his hand. He took a breath so deep that his shoulders moved with it. When he spoke, his voice was again quite normal. He said he supposed he had not been clear. He said he would be as explicit as he could. He said he had not been at the lake when the accident happened. He had been at a medical meeting in the White Mountains. He had returned to help in the search for his wife's body, to be there when her body was found. His voice as he spoke was very level.

He had heard, from Halley himself—from those who from other boats, from the club beach, had seen what happened—that Carla had collided with something, presumably a floating piece of wood, and been thrown into the water. It was the sort of thing that happened often. She had let go the towline as she fell, and Halley had circled the fast little boat to pick her up. As he circled, he had seen her sink under the water. And, when he reached the place, he had seen blood in the water—seen it only for an instant, before it disappeared. He had dived for her—and dived again. And men from other boats had dived.

There was an outcropping of rock there, just under the surface of the water. What had happened seemed obvious. It was a tragic, meaningless accident in the sparkling water of Lake Carabec on a pretty summer afternoon.

Halley had blamed himself; they had told him he was not to blame. Brian Perry had told him he must not blame himself.

Perry threw his cigarette into the fire. The fire was burning well, now. It flickered on both their faces. Perry's was without expression. It remained so as he went on.

'Until about two weeks ago,' Perry said, and spoke very slowly, very carefully, 'that was what I thought it was—a tragic accident. Then—Margaret told me the truth. She stumbled into it. I don't suppose she would have told me, otherwise. She was trying to give me the picture about John. She said something about "since that awful thing he did to your—" and then stopped. But then she had to go on, of course.'

Brian Perry took another deep breath.

'Carla didn't strike her head when she fell,' he said. 'She was all right—swimming and waiting to be picked up. Probably she was laughing. She laughed a good deal. Halley ran her down. With the boat—going very fast. She was swimming toward him and he ran her down. Nobody saw the boat strike her. Nobody was close enough to see. He ran into her and—hurt her. And then she drowned.'

He stared into the fire. He seemed to be reliving a sunny summer day.

'Halley told his wife this? She told you?'

Perry nodded.

'The urge to confess,' he said. 'To—share

guilt. I suppose it was, subconsciously, the same need which led her to tell me.'

'Doctor,' Heimrich said, 'are you saying that Halley did this intentionally? With murder in his mind?'

There was a long pause. Then Perry spoke very slowly.

'I don't know,' he said. 'Margaret says he still insisted it was an accident—that he miscalculated. He may have lied to her. She may have lied to me. As I say, she stumbled into telling me. She may have wanted to—to make it as easy for me as she could. Leave it still an accident. I—well, captain, I came here to find out.'

Heimrich waited.

'No,' Perry said, 'I didn't find out. I wouldn't have killed him. I suppose you think I might have. Whichever way it was, I wouldn't have killed him. But—I had to know. Or, I thought I did. It doesn't seem so important now, for some reason. I suppose because he's dead.'

Captain Heimrich closed his eyes.

'Would Halley have had any reason to kill your wife, doctor?' he asked.

Again, Brian Perry, leaning forward in his chair, lighted a cigarette before he answered.

'You go to the heart of the matter, don't you?' he said. 'No, captain. None that I know of. But—it was that I felt, yesterday—and when I told Margaret I'd come—it was that I felt I had to know.' And then he said, 'John was very attractive to women. He always had been. Getting older didn't seem to change that.'

For some time neither said anything. Then Heimrich said, 'Women like Miss Latham?'

'All kinds,' Perry said. 'At least, many kinds, apparently.' He looked at Heimrich for a moment, steadily. 'He was not a particularly faithful husband,' Brian Perry said. 'You've apparently found that out.'

'And his wife?'

'How did she take it? I imagine, with philosophy. Perhaps—with pity.'

Heimrich waited. He made his waiting evident.

'If you meant something else about her,' Perry said. 'I'm afraid I can't help you, captain.'

CHAPTER SEVEN

The scene should, Lynn thought, be one of beauty—the gentle, yet gay, light of candles in the long room; the firelight adding its warmer color; here and there the slow pulsation of a cigarette's glow. Tom Kemper had drawn the curtains, shutting out the storm. (But the storm was not defeated; the wind could find a way in around old windows, between the boards of the old floor.) The candle flames moved in air currents; it was as if, scattered through the room, the candles danced. One had only to close the mind to find the scene charming; had only to achieve a detachment from storm outside and—and from this strained misery within. Lynn's mind would not close; detachment could not be achieved.

Yet, she did feel herself detached, as if she looked on this through the eyes of a stranger. To a degree, this was true in the literal sense. Except for Margaret Halley, with whom her relation was a special one, not primarily of friendship, these people still remained strangers to her. Struthers Boyd, who had seemed so soggily to have had too much to drink, and had then, as if by an act of will, become sober and competent—what did she know of Boyd? Or of Tom Kemper, who was, she thought, somewhat older than he had first appeared to be, who seemed the least perturbed of any of them—and who had, after Brian Perry had gone out with Heimrich, moved closer to Audrey Latham and smiled down at her, encouragingly. What did she know of Tom Kemper—except that, standing so, attentive, he had unquestionable charm?

She knew no more of Audrey Latham—who was pretty and blond (and, Lynn still thought, although now no longer with much envy, the height a woman ought to be) and who, although the sweater she wore looked heavy enough, stayed close to the fire. Pretty and blond and young enough—and frightened.

125

Fear showed in her face. Well, that was understandable. One of those with her in the house was a murderer. But the girl managed, fleetingly, to return Tom Kemper's smile.

I should be afraid, too, Lynn thought. But she was not. It was, she supposed, part of feeling herself a stranger to the others; feeling herself not really a part of what had happened, what still was happening. Audrey must be, somehow, a part of it, since she was so clearly frightened. She had been, at least to some extent, a protégée of John Halley's. Perhaps, Lynn thought, more than that—the word was sometimes used as an euphemism. Perhaps what appeared to be fear on the girl's face was really grief.

Margaret Halley sat and looked into the fire, and the expression on her finely modelled, intelligent face was one of intentness. Perhaps, Lynn thought, she was merely remembering. Lynn could not guess. But she had never, really, tried to guess anything about Dr Halley. The circumstances of their relationship had made that inappropriate. It was for Margaret Halley to understand her, for her to assist that understanding as she could.

'No,' she said, when Kemper left Audrey and came to her, and looked at her glass, which remained almost full. 'I don't think so, thank you.'

'Keep off the chill,' Kemper said, lightly.

She merely shook her head. She did not want

126

to drink. And nothing she could drink would keep off the chill—not this chill. She discovered that she was shivering. Unquestionably, the house was cooling off, in spite of fires, of oil stoves, of the gas range burning in the distant kitchen.

He was keeping Brian a long time in the other room. She wondered why. Surely, Brian Perry could tell him nothing about—about the thing the heavy, dogged man (she still thought of him so, although Brian had said that was not enough to know about him) wanted facts about. It was not possible that Brian could know anything. He might guess much; have theories about a good many things. She thought he had. He had worked out the trick with the electricity—at least *a* trick with electricity; whether or not one actually turned—quickly and logically. He had that kind of a mind, she thought. He could not, of course, be in any way—

But—he had said that this might be—what was the word?—'important' to him. Because Halley had drowned in the lake. In, he had said, 'this lake.' As if about *this* lake there were—

Audrey Latham moved away from the fire. As if aimlessly, she moved toward Lynn's chair; unexpectedly, she sat on the arm of the chair, her head close to Lynn's. And then she said, very softly, 'Can I talk to you a minute?' and, even while Lynn looked at her, puzzled,

127

walked away toward the far end of the room—the end most distant from the fire, nearest the door which led to the rear of the house. After a moment, Lynn stood up and followed her. And, for no reason, except that it seemed to be expected, moved casually, as if without destination. When she reached the blond girl, Audrey suddenly took both of Lynn's arms in her hands.

'Listen,' she said, and her voice was still low, but was very tense. 'Listen. You've got a car, haven't you?'

'Yes,' Lynn said.

'Couldn't we get away?' Audrey said. 'Tell me—couldn't we get through? Get into the town—what's the name of the town?'

'Katonah,' Lynn said. 'I don't think we'd—'

'I can't stay here,' Audrey said. 'I've got—got something important to do. A man to see. About a contract. It's terribly important that I see this man. *Terribly!* If only—'

Lynn was shaking her head. The blond girl stopped.

'We'd never get through,' Lynn said. 'Even with chains—and I haven't got chains.'

'You don't understand,' Audrey said, and her hands tightened on Lynn's arms. 'It's—it's *vital*. Absolutely vital I—'

'My dear,' Lynn said, 'we wouldn't get out of the drive. Surely you realize that. Even if they—if they would let us go. Can't you reach this man on the telephone—I think it's still

128

working—tell him about the storm—about—?'

She did not finish because Audrey let her hands fall to her sides; for seconds stood so, in an attitude which seemed one of defeat.

'I suppose you're right,' she said. 'I suppose we couldn't. I'll try to get him on the telephone. I suppose that's the only—'

She did not finish. She walked back through the room and stood again near the fire. After a moment, she found a chair and turned it toward the fire, and sat in it. She did not go into the hall, to the telephone.

Lynn walked back toward her chair. She became conscious, then, that the other solid man—the sergeant—was standing at the far end of the room, near the curtained windows, and that he had been watching them. But, she thought, in sudden realization, he's watching all of us. She expected the sergeant, after she had sat down again in the same chair, to come to her and ask what Audrey had wanted, since he could not have heard what the blond girl said. But he did not leave his place near the windows.

Tom Kemper went to the fireplace. He rearranged the fire; added two logs to it and then, briefly, poked at it. It began to crackle again. Kemper went to sit on his heels near Audrey Latham's chair, and she turned to look at him. If they spoke, it was so softly that Lynn, not far away, could hear nothing. Boyd, carrying a drink, walked to Sergeant Forniss at the end of the room by the windows, and he did say something, but Lynn could not hear what he said, and did not try to. (What could Brian have to tell Captain Heimrich that would take so long?)

Then Brian came to the door from the central hall and stood for a moment looking around the dimly lighted room. He went to Margaret Halley and said that the captain would like to talk to her, if she felt up to it. That Lynn heard, and saw Margaret turn slowly in her chair and look up at Brian Perry. Kemper stood up and said, not trying to keep his voice low, 'She doesn't know anything. Can't he leave her alone?'

'It's quite all right, Tom,' she said. 'He's doing what he thinks he has to do.'

She got up, then—a slender, erect woman who, in this light, looked much younger than Lynn knew her to be. Kemper walked with her to the door and through it. After a moment he returned.

'Why won't he admit John killed himself?' Kemper said, and looked around the room at the others; spoke generally, it seemed, to all of them. No one answered him. Brian Perry shrugged, briefly, and crossed the room to Lynn and stood looking down at her. He looked at her intently for some seconds and then he said, as if he were speaking to himself, 'Yes, I suppose that's what it comes to.' He pulled a light chair toward him and sat in it, facing Lynn and still looking at her.

'What is it?' she said. 'What what comes to?'

He smiled, then. After a moment, he took off his glasses.

'We'll go into it another time, perhaps,' he said. 'Why did Margaret ask you here, Lynn?'

'Why?' she repeated. 'I don't know. To provide another woman, I suppose. That's an odd question, isn't it?'

'Yes,' he said. 'It's a very odd question. It was the first thing the captain asked me. You didn't know John well, did you, Lynn?'

'Hardly at all,' she said.

'So,' he said, 'had nothing against him?'

'No,' she said. 'Of course not. Did Captain Heimrich ask you that, too?'

'In effect,' he said. 'Although he apparently knew already.' He hesitated. 'We'll go into that another time, too,' he said. 'Assuming—' He finished only with a shrug.

The telephone bell rang in the hall.

Kemper went across the room toward the door, but he stopped in it and stood there for a moment. Then he turned and came back.

'That's quick work, sergeant,' Heimrich said. His voice came quite clearly into the room. He was, evidently, making no effort to speak unheard. 'Start with—' He stopped. 'The first name I gave you,' he said. 'I realize it's a bad day for that sort of thing, naturally.'

He did not speak again for a minute or more.

131

Then he said, 'Very nice work, sergeant. The next one?'

He listened more briefly. He said, 'I supposed that. Go ahead, sergeant.' This time he listened for several minutes. During that time, no one in the living room spoke. Heimrich said, 'Thanks. You've been very helpful. Still snowing there?' He listened. 'Until about midnight? Well, that's something.' They could hear the receiver replaced. Heimrich went back into the dining room, and they could hear the door close behind him.

'Checking up on us,' Brian said. 'In New York, I suppose. Have you many secrets, my dear?'

'No,' Lynn said. 'No secrets. Oh—Miss Latham is very anxious to get back to New York. But that's not a secret. She wanted me to drive her to Katonah. I told her we'd never get through.'

'No,' he said. 'You certainly couldn't. And—I don't suppose be let, in any case. What's the lady's hurry?'

She told him what she had been told.

'An odd day for it,' he said. 'New Year's Day is normally one for—repentance. Not business engagements.'

'Did she need a reason?' Lynn said. 'Wouldn't we all go if we could?'

'Yes,' he said.

The solid figure of Captain Heimrich came

into the room. Margaret Halley was not with him. Heimrich walked across the room to Struthers Boyd. Boyd went out with him.

'I think,' Dr Perry said, 'that I'll get myself a drink.' He looked at her glass. 'And freshen yours,' he said. 'I think we'll be around a while.'

*   *   *

The fire did not roar. As they reach maturity, fires in fireplaces become quiet, only now and then hissing a little as they work, sometimes crackling briefly as new logs are added. But it was a big fire by six o'clock—a fire hotly red. They could not stand close to it without discomfort. But as the fire grew, the room became colder. A few feet from the fire, they shivered, and there was dampness in the chill. The wind rattled the windows, and screamed at the house which blocked its path. A cold draft came in from the hall, and Kemper went over and closed the double doors. He came back to the fire and added another log to it. As they waited, they gradually became a tighter circle around the fire. But, even as their physical proximity increased, the real distance between the four who remained in the room after Boyd left with Heimrich seemed enhanced. Margaret Halley did not return; Sergeant Forniss remained, but he was not to be counted in the group. He remained at some distance, saying

133

nothing. Now and then he pulled back a curtain and looked out.

Brian Perry said nothing. Although he sat near her after he had brought a refilled glass, he remained, to Lynn, remote. He sat and looked into the fire, his thin, long face impassive, the reflection of firelight on his glasses hiding the expression of his eyes. Kemper, when he was not rebuilding the fire—once he left and returned after a few minutes with more wood, and with Abner Speed behind him, bringing more still—Kemper sat also, seemingly detached, and looked at the fire. But, continually, he rubbed the finger tips of his right hand with the thumb. If he would only stop doing that, Lynn found herself thinking as time passed slowly; if he would only stop! But the gesture was soundless; she was not compelled to watch it.

Audrey Latham was the most restless. She sat, hunched forward, on an ottoman near the fire; she left it to wander through the room, hugging her arms against her body. The chill drove her back and she sat on the ottoman again, at first looking around her—at Kemper, at Brian Perry, at Sergeant Forniss by the windows—and then sitting, hunched again, the palms of her hands pressed against her forehead. After a time so, she left the fire once more and again walked, restless, around the room, stopping to pull a curtain back and to look out into the swirling darkness. If she would only sit still, Lynn thought—only sit still!

After what seemed a gratingly long time, and was actually a little over half an hour, they heard someone at the double doors. They all looked toward the doors, and Struthers Boyd opened them and came in. He looked at Kemper and motioned with his thumb toward the hall and said, 'Wants you, now.'

Kemper did not move. He said, 'I've told him all I know about everything.'

Boyd shrugged. He said, 'O.K., I've passed the word.' He did not join the others by the fire. Instead, he walked the length of the room, toward the rear end and, at a window there, parted the curtains and looked out—and remained standing so, looking at what he could not see.

'Time somebody—' Kemper began, and by then Forniss had crossed the room, quickly and very silently for so large a man. He stood near Kemper's chair.

'Has to talk to everybody, Mr Kemper,' Forniss said, his voice heavy, tolerant. 'Probably won't keep you long. Just some routine questions, probably.'

Then he waited, looking at Kemper. After a moment, Kemper got up and said, 'Oh, what the hell!' and went to the doors. Forniss did not follow him, but he looked after him. Then Forniss went back to the end of the room.

The waiting went on. But one did not grow

135

accustomed to waiting, in the chilling room. Instead, in herself, Lynn felt tension building. It was time for something to happen—past time, long past time. It was time for something clean and final; it was time for an awakening from this drab, cold dream. If only, Lynn thought, the lights would come on. Only the lights again. Perhaps, she thought, at this moment a man is somewhere putting two wires together, or pulling down a switch or— Perhaps in a second, light will come on. By the time I count ten, she thought, and found that she was counting. By the time I count again to ten, she thought.

'This too will pass,' Brian Perry said, his voice low. He spoke without looking at her, but it was evident he spoke to her. 'You've done nothing about that drink.' She had not; she had put it on a table within reach, but she had not reached for it. She did now, and tasted it. It had gone flat; the glass was warm to her touch and the liquid warm, and somehow brackish, in her mouth. She put the glass back. It clinked on the polished wood of the table. The sound seemed loud.

She couldn't stand it any longer. Something had to change; her nerves screamed for change. She stood up, abruptly. Audrey Latham lifted her head from her hands and looked at Lynn; Brian Perry turned toward her. At the distant window, Struthers Boyd did not change his position.

'I'm going up and get a coat,' Lynn said, and the sound of her own voice, the disproportionate emphasis with which she spoke—startled her. Audrey continued to look at her; Brian nodded his head, slowly, and looked back at the fire. 'Is that all right?' Lynn said, across the room to Sergeant Forniss. 'Is that all right with you?'

She was saying too much; saying what did not need to be said; attaching importance to the trivial. She could not stop herself.

'Why not, Miss Ross?' Forniss said. 'No reason why not.' His voice was flat.

She went to the double doors, and opened them and then closed them behind her.

It was much colder in the hall, with doors to both living room and dining room closed. The smell of burning kerosene was harsh, acrid. She realized then that there were fumes also in the living room; that her drink had tasted of the fumes.

It was noisier in the hall; the storm seemed closer. The front door rattled with the storm, and cold air came in around it. The house creaked with the storm and somewhere, toward the rear, the wind had found an opening through which it could whistle shrilly. Lynn went up the stairs. Near the top of the flight one of the oil stoves was burning and there the odor of kerosene was pronounced. There was a faint warmth in the immediate vicinity of the stove.

She went down the hall toward her room. At the far end of the hall, beyond the door to the room, another oil stove burned. She went into the little room, and found it dark and very cold—much colder than the hall outside. On a table near the window somebody had put a candle. She lighted it. Certainly, she could not stay there, although there was relief in being alone. She would; she thought—before she remembered—fill the tub with hot water and lie in it, warming herself, washing from her body the scent of kerosene which seemed to cling to it. Then she remembered. The water would not be hot. And, there was little water. The pressure was low already, Abner Speed had said.

She opened her overnight bag and took out a perfume atomizer and sprayed scent on her sweater—sprayed much more than she had ever used before. But even the perfume, after the first few seconds, seemed to smell of kerosene. She got her suit jacket from the closet and put it on over the sweater. She moved the candle to a dressing table and, by its flickering light, straightened her hair. Then she put on lipstick. She found that doing these small, familiar things quietened her nerves a little. She began to shiver, and that was from the cold, not from nerves.

She could not stay here. It was, in a sense, a haven, but much too cold a haven. She went to the door and opened it and started out—and stopped, abruptly, and drew back.

A little way down the hall, toward the stairs, a man and a woman were standing with their arms around each other—standing so locked in each other's arms that they seemed, in the dim light, to be one person. But the man had a hand on the back of the woman's head, and was holding her head against his chest. If they heard Lynn at her door, if either of them saw her, they gave no sign. Lynn drew back into the room and closed the door, very softly. She stood looking at it.

Audrey. Audrey Latham and Tom Kemper. Holding each other like lovers, in the cold hall, the hall that reeked of kerosene fumes, that was lighted, faintly, by the oil stoves.

But that's all wrong, Lynn thought. That is—*I* must have been all wrong. I thought she and John Halley. And that Kemper was—she did not finish that, even in her mind.

But she waited. She stood for perhaps five minutes, perhaps longer, shivering in the little room. Finally—and this time with unnecessary noise, although one noise more was nothing in the creaking house, she opened the door and stepped out into the hall. The two were no longer there.

She went along the hall and down the stairs, and into the living room. Audrey and Tom Kemper were there, with the others. Audrey was by the fire, facing the rest; Kemper was some distance away, at a window, looking out.

All of them kept looking out at the storm, Lynn thought. There was a kind of compulsion to look out into the storm. Even the sergeant— She looked toward the window by which Sergeant Forniss had stood. He was not where he had been. Instead, in much the same position, Trooper Crowley was standing there.

* * *

Sergeant Forniss said there was nothing that helped particularly. He and Captain Heimrich sat in front of the fire in the dining room. The fire there was smaller. Heimrich leaned forward and poked at it; he pulled one log down toward the front; so providing space for a new log.

'They've found the break,' Forniss said. 'One of them, anyway. Tree down on the wires. Got a crew on it.'

'Any idea how long?'

'Nope,' Forniss said. 'Maybe tonight, if nothing else goes. Maybe some time tomorrow. One thing, it's pretty local. Around here. Of course, it's off in Lewisboro. Pretty much always it's off in Lewisboro.'

Heimrich's pause changed the subject.

'The girls are getting fidgety,' Forniss said. 'Miss Latham. Miss Ross. Pacing the floor a bit, the blonde is. Goes in and out, too. And Miss Ross suddenly decided she needed to get a coat. It's getting cold in there, but not as close to the fire as she was. Kemper keeps the fire going. Brings up more wood. Uses a lot of kindling to hurry it along.'

Heimrich closed his eyes.

'The doctor—Dr Perry, I mean—just sits and looks at the fire. Boyd came back after you talked to him and looked out the window. I figured you didn't make him happy.'

'No,' Heimrich said, 'I'm afraid I didn't, Charlie. There's nothing very definite, but the boys think he cuts corners. Nothing they can get him on. But—Halley had invested a nice sum in one of his projects. I have a hunch it went sour, or is going sour. It may be Halley wanted his money back. Boyd denies that, of course. Admits the investment by Halley, though.'

Heimrich opened his eyes and looked at the fire.

'Boyd was surprised to be invited here,' Heimrich said. 'At least, I think he was. Of course, he says he was at loose ends, with his wife in Florida, and that Mrs Halley took pity. It's interesting, Charlie. If Mrs Halley knew about this deal. If there's anything out of line about the deal. But then, it's all interesting. Take Dr Perry. He thinks—he's been told, in fact—that Halley killed his wife.'

He told Forniss about Halley. Forniss listened. He said, 'How about the tall girl?'

'The tall girl doesn't seem in it, one way or another,' Heimrich said. 'Except—she had a

141

breakdown a couple of years ago. Mrs Halley was her psychiatrist. Pulled her out of it. There might be something there, I suppose. Take another psychiatrist to drag it out though, wouldn't you think?'

They had psychiatrists, Forniss pointed out. They hardly needed more. They needed something simple. What had New York to report about Mr Kemper?

Not a great deal, Heimrich told him. It was a bad day to get a great deal. People tended to be inaccessible on New Year's Day; if found, they tended to be grumpy. The best way to describe Kemper, apparently, was that he was an extra man; the sort of young man who was available when needed; who could always find the time for a summer weekend, a winter skiing party, when there was a risk that women would unduly predominate.

'Young?' Forniss said, with doubt.

It was a manner of speaking, Heimrich agreed. Young enough, at any rate, for women a little older; boyish and bright enough and charming; a man who would earn holidays by thoughtful little actions—if a tennis court needed marking, there was Tom Kemper, marker in hand, and a cheerful smile; if there was an errand to be done in a nearby village, there was Tom, more than ready to drive in and do it.

'In somebody else's car?' Forniss said.

'Now Charlie,' Heimrich said. 'Yes, I

142

suppose so. A great help to hostesses.'

Forniss thought that Kemper might be getting a little old for that. Did Kemper appear to have other occupation?

Apparently, he did not—but, again, it was a bad day for enquiries. Apparently he had money from some source. Enough money for a small apartment and, probably, a good wardrobe. Enough, in the minor matters of tab picking-up, to get along.

'At a guess,' Heimrich said, 'a small income—and friends with better incomes. Women a little older than he, probably. Women who appreciate little attentions.'

It did not, Forniss said, seem like a career with much future. It seemed like an occupation one might grow out of. 'Like a tennis player,' Forniss said.

'Yes,' Heimrich said. 'A little like a tennis player.'

'Mrs Halley?' Forniss said.

'Probably,' Heimrich said. 'Quite probably, Charlie.'

'I did notice,' Forniss said, 'that he's a great man for keeping the fires burning. And offering people drinks. Knows where everything is. He didn't want to come talk to you. I had to look at him.'

'Yes,' Heimrich said. 'I gathered that. Thinks the whole business is an imposition. On Mrs Halley, chiefly. Thinks we ought to call it suicide like she does, and get out from under

143

foot. Meanwhile, doesn't know anything about anything. The young women are getting restless, you say?'

'Yep,' Forniss said. 'The blond one, especially.'

'Good,' Heimrich said.

'The blond girl wanted the tall girl to do something,' Forniss said. 'Led her off and asked her. Got turned down, from the way they acted. I don't know what. Of course, the tall girl—'

'Miss Ross,' Heimrich said.

'Miss Ross has got a car. The other one might have thought it was a good day for a ride. To the station, for example.'

'Wouldn't be, would it?' Heimrich said. 'Very bad day. Is Miss Latham frightened, Charlie? Of—oh, the storm? The fact that the power's off? Or—of anything else?'

Forniss thought a moment.

'Yep,' he said. 'It could be that's it. It could be of us, of course.'

'Yes,' Heimrich said. 'Mrs Halley says Miss Latham lied to us, Charlie. Oh, not about what she saw. About her relationship with Mr Halley. Or, perhaps didn't lie. Perhaps merely misunderstood. Mrs Halley likes to see all sides of things. Very proper, in her profession.'

Forniss waited.

Heimrich had, he told Forniss, asked Mrs Halley first about the relationship of her dead husband and Miss Latham. He had told

144

Margaret Halley what the girl said. And Mrs Halley had said, 'The poor thing,' and, then, that it was a little complicated. She and her husband, she said, had talked it over; they were both worried about it. The captain must try to understand.

He must try to understand that John Halley was interested in young people of talent—had always been. 'Because,' she said, 'he was one himself, once. Not a big talent. Rather a—' She had paused. 'A grace,' she said.

It had come to little; it had left him sympathetic. He had helped many, including Miss Latham, who had a pleasant talent, from which she hoped much. 'I'm afraid too much,' Margaret Halley said. 'John had begun to think so.'

At first, Mrs Halley was sure, Miss Latham had understood Halley's purpose. But later— well, it was kindest to think that she had misunderstood. 'Perhaps,' Margaret Halley said, 'she began to be a little discouraged about her work. Sought something else, and convinced herself that there was something else. And—John was always very attractive to women.'

It became apparent that Miss Latham was attracted; thought her feelings returned. (This was the most probable explanation. It was also, obviously, possible that Miss Latham had been less ingenuous. It was better to think the best of people.) This had worried Halley; he had talked it over with his wife. They had agreed that he should disentangle himself; that it was not fair to the girl to let her misunderstand.

'Very understanding herself, Mrs Halley is,' Heimrich said. Forniss raised his eyebrows. 'No,' Heimrich said, 'I don't, Charlie. There are all sorts of possibilities, obviously. Miss Latham may have told the truth, and Halley lied to his wife. His wife may have believed him. She may not have. She may be telling us what she thinks was true. And, she may not. Also, it may have been as she says, which wouldn't be unusual, either.'

'Halley may have been walking out on the girl,' Forniss said. Heimrich nodded. 'Or on his wife.' Heimrich nodded again. 'Things like that upset women sometimes,' Forniss said. Heimrich agreed that such things often upset women. 'It wouldn't take much strength to hit a man on the head with a rock,' Forniss said. 'Particularly if he'd already begun to get the effects of the barbiturate.' Heimrich agreed it would not. 'And,' Forniss said, 'Miss Latham and Mrs Halley were both up and around last night.'

'Yes,' Heimrich said. 'Mrs Halley doesn't deny that. Has a very simple explanation, though. Went down to see if her husband was still awake. Found he wasn't there and went back upstairs and to bed. Never went near the basement. If Miss Latham says she saw her, she

146

supposes Miss Latham did. But, she wasn't carrying anything. If Miss Latham says she was, Miss Latham is mistaken. She's afraid poor Latham often doesn't get things straight.'

Forniss waited. Heimrich added the details of Margaret Halley's account.

She had, as she had said previously, gone to bed and, lightly, to sleep. She and John Halley had occupied separate rooms. They usually did in the country, although not in town. She had awakened several times. Finally, since she had not heard him come up, she had put on a robe and gone down to the living room. She had found it empty. Relieved, she had gone back upstairs and gone to bed, and to sleep.

'Noticed he hadn't drunk his rum punch?'

'Yes. She says so. Decided to leave it till morning. For Mrs Speed.'

'Didn't have a look into his bedroom?'

'No,' Heimrich said. 'Because the door squeaks. Halley slept very lightly, and once he waked up it took him a long time to get back to sleep. Sometimes he didn't get back to sleep at all. That's what the sleeping pills were for.'

'And,' Forniss said, 'the man was full of barbiturate when he drowned. Ask her about that?'

Heimrich shook his head.

'Not yet,' he said.

'She could have put the stuff in his rum punch,' Forniss said. 'Only he didn't drink the rum punch. Unless Mrs Speed's lying.'

147

'No,' Heimrich said. 'I don't think she's lying, Charlie.'

'So,' Forniss said. 'The rum punch's out.'

Apparently, Heimrich agreed, the rum punch was out. It was rather a pity, naturally. But there it was.

'But,' Heimrich said, 'he did drink whiskey—scotch and soda, as Kemper and Boyd remember it. After the toast to the New Year. Readily soluble in alchohol, Nembutal is. And—seems the others stuck to champagne, so there wouldn't have been the risk of getting the stuff in the wrong drink. And—who do you suppose was tending bar, Charlie? Part of the evening, anyway?'

Forniss considered, briefly. Then he said, 'Kemper. Being helpful around the house?'

'No,' Heimrich said. 'Mr Boyd. Thought his old school chum looked tired. Took over for him. Very thoughtful man, Mr Boyd. But it could have been put in any time, naturally. Party like that, people walk around, leave their drinks, go back to them.'

'And,' Forniss said, 'still may have taken it himself. And, when he got down to the lake, decided not to wait for the stuff to work.'

'Yes,' Heimrich said. 'Killed himself twice. People do, you know. Take poison. Then jump out windows. Also—he may have been killed twice.' Heimrich sighed. He said that that happened too. Only it was, usually, a case of try, try again.

148

'If at first you don't succeed,' Heimrich said. 'But here, there would have been success the first time.' He closed his eyes. 'Of course,' he said, "there's also the one about not letting the right hand know what the left hand's doing, isn't there?'

There was a knock at the door, and the door was immediately opened. Mrs Speed said there was food in the living room. 'Such as it is,' she said.

CHAPTER EIGHT

Now there was a table at one end of the long room, and there was food on the table. Mrs Speed had brought the food in from the kitchen, and, as she arranged it, the table had taken on an incongruously festive air. There was a turkey. There was a ham. There were bowls of salad and plates of cheese. This food was to have been eaten as it was needed, in a bright warm room, after eggnog, on the afternoon of New Year's Day. But now the room was cold—increasingly cold. The sound of the wind was loud in the room, and the candles flickered in draft; the tiny flames of the candles leaned far out, as if seeking escape. The fire did more than the candles to light the room, but much of the room remained in shadow.

Mrs Speed put the food on the table, and looked at it for a moment and then said, 'I guess that's everything,' and looked at Margaret Halley.

'Thank you,' Margaret said, in a voice without tone. 'It looks very nice, Mrs Speed.' But Margaret made no move toward the table. For some time, no one moved. It was as if they had not heard, did not see the food; as if they had grown too numb for effort.

It was Tom Kemper, finally, who roused himself; who said, in a quite ordinary voice, which was, for that very reason, as incongruous as the gayety of the table, that they had better eat before everything got cold. 'As cold as we are,' he said and then, to Audrey Latham, who was nearest him, 'Come on. Let's get something.' He walked over to the table and began to carve the turkey and, after a moment, Audrey got up and followed him and took a plate from the stack of plates and stood looking at it as if she could not decide its purpose. Then Brian Perry touched Lynn's arm and she had nodded, and they both got up. They walked from the fireplace, which was near the mid-point of the inner wall of the long room, down the room to the table. As they walked, the others—Margaret Halley, Boyd, the two already at the table—watched them as if there were something strange, meaningful, in the progress of a tall man and a tall girl through a room toward a table of food.

It was then that Lynn first realized how curiously wary they had all become. It was as if, to each of the six, the movements of each of the others were to be observed, considered, searched for some meaning under the surface of the movement, or of the words. (Had Kemper meant more than he said in saying that the food would grow as cold as they were? Did it mean something that he had made the first movement toward food, and had taken Audrey with him?) They watched, and listened, for the significant—for the inimical. That was it, Lynn thought, sitting with a plate on her lap, eating food she could not taste. Each felt threatened by the others; the most commonplace action might conceal danger.

And it was, of course, absurd. Accept what Captain Heimrich asserted—that one of them was a murderer. That one was then alone endangered and alone needed to be cautious, and watchful. The rest had only to wait, with what resignation they could manage, until, in some way not now clear, Captain Heimrich made up his mind.

He seemed in no hurry about it. He ate his dinner, sitting with Sergeant Forniss, at the end of the room nearest the front windows, quite close to the shrouded sofa. They sat at a small table and appeared to eat with pleasure. But it was, nevertheless, evident that they, too, watched. Probably it was the consciousness of Heimrich's watchfulness which had so alerted the others. After they had all eaten, Heimrich would go back to his dogged questioning, and even that would be preferable to this—this suspension in cold fog.

But, when they had finished, Forniss took his plate and Heimrich's, both plates cleaned neatly, and put them on the end of the table reserved for used dishes, and then went back and sat down again. And when they had all finished, and merely sat waiting, Heimrich still did nothing—except watch. Lynn tried to see what he was seeing. Perhaps, she thought, that is what we are all doing.

Margaret sat near the fire, its light giving color to her set face. She had accepted the plate of food Tom Kemper brought her, but she did not seem to have eaten any of it. After a few minutes, she got up and returned the plate to the table, and went back to her chair. As she moved through the room, she looked first at one of her guests and then at another.

Brian Perry ate, slowly, not seeming conscious of what he did. He watched the others, too. But where Audrey, and Kemper also, looked quickly and then away again (as if to watch were in itself a risk) Brian looked long and thoughtfully at each in turn, and finally at Lynn. Then, for the first time, he smiled. 'We're all very edgy,' he said, quietly. 'I imagine that's his idea.' The faintest motion of head indicated Captain Heimrich. 'He's rather like a cat,' Brian said. 'A waiting cat.'

Boyd was drinking again, with dinner finished, coffee served. He took the brandy Kemper offered and, when he had finished, took the small round glass back to the portable bar and again filled it. They all watched as he did this; followed him with their eyes from chair to bar, back to chair again. After a time, Audrey Latham began to move about the room, as she had moved earlier. They watched her.

Forniss got up and went to one of the windows which looked out toward the road. He stood there for a moment, looking at something, and then they all heard, above the storm, the sound of a heavy truck motor. Outside, when Forniss stepped aside, but still held the curtain back, they could see a flashing red light.

'Plow,' Forniss said, and let the curtain fall. But then Kemper and Brian Perry went to the window, and after a time Lynn joined them. A truck with red lights flashing rhythmically was moving slowly along the road. As it moved, it threw snow up, which the truck's light brightened. The falling snow seemed less thick.

'Must figure it's about over,' Kemper said, and seemed to speak very loudly, although his voice was not really loud. Nobody replied. Audrey Latham, whose nervous wandering had taken her to the far end of the room, came its length to join them. She watched the moving truck. She said, 'Oh. But we could get out now, couldn't we?' She faced Heimrich. 'Couldn't we?' she repeated, her tone demanding answer.

'The road's passable,' Heimrich said. 'Or will be. You're very anxious to leave, Miss Latham?'

'Who wouldn't be?' she said. 'Who wouldn't be, captain? You mean—we have to stay here?'

'Nobody's under arrest,' Heimrich said. 'But one is a murderer. For the rest, it's merely an inconvenience, Miss Latham.'

Forniss dropped the curtain. They waited, in the still room—still except for the sighing of the wind outside; a faint whistling sound from the fire—for Heimrich to go on. But he said nothing more. Boyd got up and once more refilled his glass. With it, he walked to Margaret Halley's chair and, leaning down, said something to her which the others could not hear. She listened; she shook her head. Boyd went to his own chair. But almost at once he quitted it and went out of the room into the hall. Heimrich watched him. They all watched him. Abruptly, Audrey Latham crossed the room and went after Struthers Boyd. They watched her, too.

'How long are you going to keep us here, captain?' Kemper said. 'You don't deny you are keeping us?'

'Now Mr Kemper,' Heimrich said. 'I'd rather you all stayed. Simpler that way. It wouldn't make too much difference in the long run, of course.'

'You've nothing to go on,' Kemper said. 'Not even enough to make it murder. What do you expect to get?'

'Character,' Heimrich said. 'Among other things. The character to fit the crime.'

'Oh for God's sake!' Kemper said, and walked away. Lynn and Brian Perry stood with the detectives and watched him go. Perry turned to Heimrich. He said, 'Is that the way you do it?'

'One of the ways, doctor,' Heimrich said. 'Also, of course, no situation remains static. Not indefinitely.'

'As any cat knows,' Brian said. Heimrich opened his blue eyes very widely.

'Cat?' he said. 'Why a cat, doctor?'

'Watch,' Brian said. 'Until the prey thinks the cat's asleep. Until it moves. Comes too near.'

'Yes,' Heimrich said. 'Well, I'm just a policeman, doctor. Looking for a murderer. A man who tricked another man into going down to the lake. So he could kill him and push him in.'

'A man?'

'Manner of speaking, doctor,' Heimrich said. 'You've something you want to tell me?'

'No,' Perry said. 'I wasn't your man, captain.'

'No,' Heimrich said, without inflection. 'But, it was your simile, doctor. A cat waiting. Until the cat's time comes.'

Heimrich did not, now, make any effort to lower his voice. He could be heard by all in the room. Kemper, who was across the room, listened. Margaret Halley did not move, but she could hear. Lynn was sure she listened, too.

'Until it was time to kill,' Heimrich said. 'Because of hatred. Or in rage, which is somewhat different. Or for profit, naturally.'

'John's money comes to me,' Margaret said, her voice quite clear, and quite without expression. She did not turn from her regard of the fire. 'Do you mean that?'

'Now Dr Halley,' Heimrich said. 'I supposed it did. But there are other ways of profiting. Aren't there, Mr Boyd?'

Lynn had not seen that Boyd had returned. He stood in the doorway, listening.

'Afraid I don't get you, friend,' Boyd said. ''Fraid I don't know what you're shooting at.'

'Ways of making a profit,' Heimrich said. 'Direct. Or indirect. By murder, in this case.'

'My husband,' Margaret said, 'killed himself. You'll never prove anything else.'

'Oh yes,' Heimrich said. 'I think I will, doctor. One of you will tell me. In one way or another.' He paused. 'I think more than one of you knows. Or guesses. May even have seen something. It can be risky to know too much—in a dark house. A large dark house.'

'Nonsense,' Margaret said. 'You're talking nonsense, captain.'

'She's right,' Kemper said. 'You're getting

156

nowhere. Why don't you drop it, captain?'

'Now Mr Kemper,' Heimrich said. 'They wouldn't like me to drop it, you know.'

Boyd came into the room. He moved over to the bar, and picked up a bottle. Kemper joined him there and Lynn thought they talked, briefly. But they were at the other end of the room, and it was not even certain that they talked, as they bent together over the bar. Then Audrey Latham came back into the room.

'Oh—Miss Latham,' Heimrich said, and then everybody looked at her. 'There are one or two points you might help us on.'

'*No!*' she said; and the word was an exclamation. 'I've told you all I can. All I saw last night.' She paused. 'On the stairs,' she said.

'Nevertheless,' Heimrich said, and walked over to stand beside Audrey. He looked very large, beside the slim blond girl. 'A point or two you might clear up.'

He waited. She looked up at him. She sighed deeply. 'In the dining room,' Heimrich said. She went out into the hall. Heimrich started to follow her. Then he turned.

'The murder was unnecessary,' he said. He looked around at them. 'You may as well know that. One of you couldn't let dead enough alone.'

Then he followed Audrey Latham.

* * *

Heimrich had not told Audrey Latham what he meant. He had talked to her briefly; not for longer than fifteen minutes. 'Nothing about that,' Audrey told Lynn. 'I'm sure I don't know what he meant.' She paused. 'For my money,' she said, 'he's a very stupid man.'

She and Lynn shared a bed, in the room which had been Audrey's. It was Margaret Halley who had suggested it. But it had, unexpectedly, been Brian Perry who had brought the problem up; he who had said to Lynn, when, quite early in the evening, Heimrich had indicated that, for the time being, he had nothing more to ask of any of them, that she couldn't keep warm under an electric blanket when there was no electricity. Mrs Halley, who had remained in some distant world of her own, had then returned from it, briefly, to say that, of course she couldn't and that they would find something. 'I'll have Mrs Speed get the blankets off—' she had begun, but then she had stopped; had looked at Lynn.

It was evident—too evident—what she had been about to say, and her doubt whether she should make the suggestion was equally clear. John Halley's bed had had blankets on it; John Halley would not be needing the blankets. It was quite reasonable; a quite practical solution. But, before it was made, Lynn was shaking her head. So, it was not made.

'Couldn't you and Audrey move in together?' Margaret Halley said, instead. 'It's a double bed. I don't know quite what else to suggest.'

There had been a momentary pause. Then Audrey Latham had said, 'Of course. If Lynn doesn't—'

Lynn found that, to some slight degree, she did mind. But it was only habit, she told herself—the relaxed habit of a bed to oneself. 'Of course,' Lynn said, and smiled at Audrey, and said something about their keeping one another warm—something which, in her own ears, sounded meaningless. Audrey had, then, said that she would go on and 'straighten things up a little,' and had gone up. Lynn had given her time; had gone up in half an hour to find the blond girl in the double bed, wearing a woolen robe, propped on pillows, smoking a cigarette by the light of a flickering candle.

'The first warm place I've been in in hours,' Audrey said. 'This dreadful house!'

But she seemed, to Lynn, more relaxed than she had been, and less fearful.

'I brought your pillows in from the other room,' Audrey said. 'And your night bag, while I was about it.'

This was a little surprising. It had not occurred to Lynn that Audrey Latham was one of those who do small, thoughtful things for others. Lynn said, with the utmost conventionality, that Audrey shouldn't have, and went into the bathroom to brush her teeth. She started, then, to go to the other room for her robe, saying she was going to. 'Brought that in, too,' Audrey said. 'Aren't I the perfect hostess?'

She was indeed, Lynn told her, only partly undressing—shiveringly undressing—putting the robe on.

It was, after a few seconds, comfortably warm in the bed. Audrey put an ash tray between them.

'Will I ever be glad to get out of here,' Audrey said. 'Was there ever such a weekend?'

Not often, Lynn said. Not often she hoped. She shivered. It was then she asked Audrey if Heimrich had explained what he meant. 'It was a strange thing to say,' Lynn said.

'Personally,' Audrey said. 'I think it was a curtain line. Unless poor John—' She did not finish. 'All he wanted from me was, did I know John was—was breaking up our arrangement. I said, how could I, when he wasn't?' She stubbed out her cigarette and turned to look at Lynn, who just perceptibly shook her head.

'You're a baby, aren't you?' Audrey said, and spoke tolerantly. 'There's no secret about it, now. What's the way they put it, speaking nicely? I was poor John's protégée. The way they mean it. I told this dumb policeman. That and—other things.' She looked at Lynn intently, as if she had made everything clear. 'More than I wish now I had. But, I was worked up. Don't you ever get worked up?'

'Yes,' Lynn said. 'Oh, yes.'

'Of course,' Audrey said. 'Weren't you once—I mean didn't you sort of go—' She stopped. She said she talked too much.

'Yes,' Lynn said. 'I did sort of go off. But that was quite a while ago. You needn't—'

'Now don't get me wrong,' Audrey said. 'I talk too much.' For some seconds, then, she did not talk at all. Then she said, reflectively, 'Too damn much,' and added, 'I don't mean to you, my dear.' She paused again, and then said, 'Well, we live and learn, don't we?'

'Did he mean that Mr Halley was ill? Would have died anyway?'

'Don't ask me,' Audrey said. 'If you ask me, Heimrich would believe anything. Anything the right people told him. But, you know how they are. Cops, I mean.'

'No,' Lynn said. 'I don't, really.'

'Not that I've had anything to do with them,' Audrey said, rather quickly. 'Don't think that. But, anybody can read the papers. Shakedowns. People with money treated one way. Other people, another way.' She was again silent for a minute or more. 'You know what,' she said, then, 'it could be he's dumb enough to think I killed John. Because John was walking out on me—not that he was, really. Can you picture that?'

She turned and looked at Lynn fully. She was very pretty, Lynn thought. She had very large blue eyes. At the moment they seemed to brim with innocence.

161

'Of course not,' Lynn said. 'Actually—why is he so sure Mr Halley was killed? The blanket's going off, but—perhaps the plug pulled out a little way. Perhaps I did the wrong thing. It's so—it's such a *little* thing.'

'I've never understood about that,' Audrey said. 'What did it have to do with it?'

Lynn told her the theory that Brian Perry had worked out; was told by Audrey that Brian Perry was a smart cookie.

'You've started to fall for him,' she said. 'You know that, don't you? You go sort of coo-y.'

Lynn was startled; after a second she was not greatly startled. 'Coo-y' was certainly an odd way to go; it would certainly be an odd time for it. But still—She shook her head, slightly.

'Have it your own way,' Audrey said. 'Only—I'd watch my step. That's what I'm going to do from here on in.' She stubbed out her cigarette. 'They can bet on that.'

'They?' Lynn said.

'Anybody,' Audrey said. 'Anybody can bet on that, was what I meant. What do you say we get some sleep?'

Lynn put out her cigarette. Audrey cupped a hand over the candle flame, and blew the flame out. The room was very dark; then, slowly, it was gray; objects in it could be discerned. But then the objects seemed slowly to fade into the grayness. The last thing Lynn remembered before she slept was the deep, regular breathing of the girl who lay, very quietly, beside her...

She awakened because she was no longer warm. For an instant, the night before seemed to be repeating itself, she thought, hazily. 'The blanket's gone off again.' But then she was more fully awake, and then quite fully awake, to find herself alone in the bed.

She said, 'Audrey?' and then, 'Miss Latham?' in a voice loud enough to be heard through the small room. She was not answered. The wind wailed outside. 'The bathroom,' Lynn thought, 'of course,' and waited. After a few moments she groped on the table by the bed and found a folder of matches. When she started to strike a match, she found that her hands were uncertain. She was shivering again. It was, of course, because she was cold.

Finally a match flared. The candle was still on the table and she lighted it. Slowly, objects in the room became visible—and the bathroom door. The door stood open. 'Audrey?' Lynn said, this time more loudly. When there was no answer, she got out of the bed and carried the candle to the bathroom. The bathroom was empty. She stood for a moment looking into it and then went to the closet. Her own things were there. There was nothing of Audrey Latham's.

Audrey had gone. Of course, Lynn thought. That's why she was so thoughtful; why she brought my bag in here, my robe. She had

163

taken her own bag into the room I had; put a robe on over her clothes, waited until I was asleep. She must have gone down the back stairs and—

I must tell someone, Lynn thought. Someone must stop her. She thinks because the plow got through the road is open but she'll—

CHAPTER NINE

The hall was empty, and very cold. Wind blew through it; here the sound of the wailing wind was louder than it had been in the room. The whole house seemed to be shaking with the wind. The little flame of the candle leaned far over; Lynn cupped a hand about it, and it straightened, but then again flickered wildly. She held her cupped hand closer—so close she could feel the candle's tiny warmth. But then the wind tricked her, eddied back. The candle went out.

There was still a faint light in the hallway. It came from the oil stove, near the head of the main stairway. The stove cast a small circle of light on the ceiling; splattered the floor around it with faint light.

'Audrey?' Lynn said, and for some reason spoke softly—so softly that, even as she spoke, she realized that the sound of the wind tore the word from her mouth, destroyed it. She took a

164

breath to call more loudly, but then released the breath without sound. At the far end of the hall there was, momentarily, the movement of light.

She could not see the source of the light; the light was faint, reflected. But she thought it must come from a flash. She went toward the light, down the hall, moving silently on slippered feet. When she was nearly at the end of the hall, she saw the light again—still reflected, now seemingly from a greater distance.

The light, she realized as she went down the hallway, came from the hall which ran at right angles to it, crossing the rear of the house. She called, then, more loudly—called Audrey Latham's name. She was not answered.

When she reached the hallway corner, she paused momentarily, since the rear hall— narrower than the other—was unlighted— unlighted save by the faint gray light which came through a window from half way along it. She called again, still more loudly, and still her voice mingled with the sound of the wind. She would never, she thought, outscream the wind. She would go back and—and find someone. Heimrich was somewhere in the house; the sergeant, the young trooper. She had turned to go back when she heard the sound—thought she heard the sound which was like a sob. It was very faint; it was tangled in the sound of the wind.

But then, she thought, she could not go back—take the time, waste the time, to find help in the dark and noisy house. She went along the hall, holding her arms out on either side, finding that on either side she could touch the walls with her out-reaching hands. She guided herself by the walls, down the gray formlessness of the hall.

Just in time she caught herself, held herself with hands against the walls. The hallway ended in a flight of stairs, pitching downward sharply. She swayed for an instant at the stairhead before she caught herself. She heard the sound again—the sound like a moaning sob. It came from below her.

She called once more and again was unanswered. Groping, she found handrails on either side and went down the stairs. Now and then she stopped to listen, but heard only the raging wind as it wailed around the house; heard only the house, muttering as it braced itself against the wind.

The stairway came down into a wider hall. The night's grayness seeped into it through the open door to the kitchen, beyond. There was enough light when she was near the bottom of the narrow stairs for her to see what huddled there.

Audrey Latham lay on her back, one leg twisted under her. Her eyes were open; her face unmarred.

Lynn drew in a shuddering breath as she

crouched beside the small, blond girl and then, seeing, put one hand up toward her face, as if to ward off what she saw. The blond head lay in a darkness darker than the floor; the hair was matted by the darkness. And—the girl was alive. There was life—hurt, stunned life—in the open eyes.

Lynn bent toward her and said the girl's name and the eyes answered and then the lips answered, if a moan is an answer. Lynn crouched and reached toward her—to touch her, to lift her up, somehow to assuage with hands the terrible hurt.

Then she heard a scuffling sound behind her and started to turn to face the sound. She did not have time to turn. Hard hands wrenched at her neck and shoulders, drew her up and then there was a great jar and a glaring redness which, almost instantly, closed darkly in upon itself and was utter black...

There was no light, yet there was some change in the quality of the darkness. Gropingly, Lynn came back to the consciousness of herself, out of the utter black which was more than darkness, which had been without the dreams of sleep. She was Lynn Ross now; Lynn Ross in a place without light. She willed to move, and her body moved; she moved her hands about her, and moved them on smooth, cold hardness. She held her hands up, but she could not see her hands.

For a cold instant she thought, *'I'm blind! I*

can't see!' Then she pressed her fingers against her eyes and felt no pain and then covered her eyes with her fingers. There was a difference—a difference almost imperceptible, but enough. She was in a dark place, but the darkness was of the place. She brought her hands slowly down her face and on the right side of her face—in the cheek, along the jaw—there was a sharp pain. She took her hand away quickly, and the sharpness of the pain diminished, but a throbbing pain remained. She waited, and the pain lessened.

It was cold where she was and then she realized another thing: it was almost quiet. She could still hear the angry wind, but now it seemed to be at a great distance—muffled, shut out. She listened, making herself listen. She heard harsh, uneven breathing which was not her own. Still, she could see nothing.

She had been lying prone. Now she raised herself on hands and knees, steadied herself so, and began to move her hands in widening circles on the floor, seeking some contact which would provide orientation. For a time her hands encountered nothing, except the smooth, cold hardness over which they traveled. Then she touched something. Her fingers closed, briefly, on the heel of a woman's shoe.

'Audrey?' Lynn said. '*Audrey?*'

A strange, quivering moan answered her.

Lynn, still on hands and knees, moved

closer—felt her way closer—felt her way closer along the girl's body, then felt the rough material of a coat. She drew herself along until she was beside the girl, who lay on her back on the floor. Then one of Lynn's groping hands, sliding in its search, was in a wetness—a wetness faintly sticky to the touch. She moved her hand a little and touched hair.

'Audrey,' she said. 'Can't you—'

And then it was light. The darkness had been complete; now the light seemed as complete as the darkness had been. She was in a place which glared with light. The light was, for that instant, as sudden, as blinding, as the blow had been. Involuntarily, Lynn put a hand—but not the hand which had been in the wetness—to her unprotected eyes. But after a second or two the light dimmed to quite ordinary light—harsh light, certainly, unkind light. But no more light than comes from a moderate-sized bulb, set unshaded in the ceiling.

She was in a quite ordinary small storeroom. The cold smoothness which had been under her hands (now she sat back on her heels, looking around her) was the smoothness of linoleum, here and there a little worn. On three sides of the room there were shelves, and cans of food were stacked on the shelves—cans of soups, of meats; bottles which held sauces. The fourth side of the room was a door. There was a handhold on the door, and above it a thumbpiece. There was nothing strange or frightening about the room—except the slight girl who lay beside her on the floor; who had turned a little, moaned again, when the light came on. Nothing but the girl, and the blood on the floor and on Lynn Ross's hand.

Audrey Latham's eyes were open, and now her lips were moving. But there was something hideously wrong, something unreally wrong, about her head. Where it rested on the floor, it seemed to rest flatly—as if there were no back to the head. Violent sickness ran through Lynn as she looked down at the girl. She fought it back. Then Audrey tried to raise herself. Kneeling beside her, Lynn put a hand under the girl's shoulders; let the crushed head rest on her arm and shoulder. Audrey tried to speak and at first unintelligible sounds—dreadful sounds—came from her lips. (And her lips, untouched, were still sweetly curved; still bright with lipstick.) The girl tried again.

'Tell him—' she said. Lynn bent closer. 'Tell—'

The effort was terrible. The whole slight body seemed to tremble with the effort.

'*Don't*,' Lynn said. 'I'll get somebody. *Don't try*—'

But the look in the staring eyes stopped her.

'—time,' Audrey said. 'Listen—' The eyes closed; opened again. The girl moaned again, the moan shaking her body. 'Listen?'

'Yes,' Lynn said. 'Yes. I'm listening.' She held the girl close, pillowing the battered head

170

on her shoulder. And blood seeped through the robe, was warm on her skin—and then was cold on her skin. 'You'll be all right,' Lynn said. 'You'll—'

'—in hand,' Audrey said. 'It hurts so—*so.*' The last word became a moan. 'Tell him—like—glass.'

Lynn waited.

She tried to fix the words in her mind—words so agonizingly spoken; to the speaker evidently so vital, so necessary. But the words meant nothing. The girl's eyes closed.

'Who?' Lynn said. 'Tell who?'

The eyes opened again; they seemed to flicker open.

'On—stairs,' Audrey said, the words so faint that Lynn could only guess at them. 'Thought—I—' The eyes closed again, and a tremor ran through the slight body. Lynn moved; started to free herself. Not these meaningless words, she thought. I've got to get somebody. Get—

'Live and learn,' Audrey said, quite clearly. 'Tell—doctor—doctor had—'

And then her body lost all resilience in Lynn's arms; became only a heavy weight. Audrey Latham bled at the mouth and died.

For a moment, Lynn held the limp body in her arms. Then, very gently, she put it down. She was herself shaking, convulsively. Slowly, she began to get to her feet. And then she saw the hatchet on the floor.

It was near the closed door. It was an old hatchet, with a rough wooden handle. It did not look sharp. But that was difficult to tell because of what was on the blade—on the whole head—of the hatchet.

Lynn did not scream. The need to scream was harsh in her throat; seemed to be a sourness in her throat. But she walked the few steps to the door quite steadily, and pressed down on the thumbpiece.

For an instant, then, when the thumbpiece resisted pressure, she thought she was locked in—locked in with death. But the latch was only stiff; she pressed harder and the latch outside lifted. She opened the door and was in the back hall. And here, too, the lights were bright. And here, as not in the closed-off storeroom, the roaring of the wind was loud. But she cried out for help, and cried above the wind. She heard the sound of men running, and leaned against one of the counters and put her head down, because blackness was beginning again to swirl around her.

Heimrich came first, and then Brian Perry. She only pointed to the open door of the storeroom. Heimrich went in, and then said, abruptly, 'Come here, doctor,' and Perry went into the little room, and crouched beside the body of Audrey Latham. He did not touch it. After a moment, he stood up again. He came out of the room and took Lynn by the shoulders, and turned her and looked into her

172

face.

'*She's dead, isn't she?*' Lynn said—heard her strange voice saying. '*She's dead, isn't she?* She said, "Live and learn" and then she died. *She said*—'

'Get hold of yourself, Lynn,' Perry said. 'Do you hear me? Get hold of yourself.'

He cupped one hand under her chin, to raise it.

'*Don't!*' Lynn said. 'It's—'

Perry looked, and swore. Then, very gently, he ran his fingers along the delicate bone of Lynn's jaw. 'All right,' he said. 'Nothing broken. You were knocked out?'

'Yes,' she said. 'I—I found her. At the foot—she's dead, isn't she? You can tell me now. I'm all right.'

'Yes,' Brian Perry said.

Heimrich came out of the storeroom. He closed the door behind him.

'How long would she have lived, doctor?' Heimrich said.

Brian Perry released Lynn. He turned to Heimrich.

'How long?' he repeated. 'I wouldn't have expected her to live at all, captain. The skull's crushed. The—the brain lacerated. Sometimes, of course—'

'She was alive,' Lynn said. 'Lying at the foot of the stairs. Moaning—and—' She took a deep breath. 'Her eyes were open,' she said. 'Then—afterward—'

173

'Wait,' Heimrich said. 'Tell me a little at a time.'

She told him—of the black which came with the blow; of awakening. She did not know how long a time had intervened. Heimrich looked at Perry.

'Not long,' Perry said. 'At least, I'd judge not. She was knocked out. Probably merely by a fist. It may have been only a few minutes. I suppose—whoever it was, dragged them both in there and closed the door. To give himself time? Time to get back to one of the rooms?'

'Now doctor,' Heimrich said. 'But, that's possible, naturally. She talked, you say—regained consciousness and talked?'

'I'm not sure she'd lost consciousness,' Lynn said. 'She—looked at me, captain.'

'Yes,' Heimrich said. 'She talked? Tried to talk?'

'She said—words,' Lynn told him. 'She said, "Tell him," but not who she meant. And something about stairs and something about a hand. Did she mean—what she was hit with?'

'I don't know, Miss Ross,' Heimrich said. 'Was that all she said?'

'She said—almost at the last—quite clearly—"Live and learn." She said, "Live and learn." And then she died.'

Lynn was conscious of long shudders which went through her body. Perry turned, quickly. He took her arms again.

'Breathe deep,' he said. 'Just breathe deep.'

And his own chest swelled; the slow breathing movement of his whole body was conveyed, through his pressing hands, to hers. 'Easy, Lynn,' he said. 'Just—easy.'

'I'm all right,' Lynn said. 'She said something about a doctor, too, she said to Heimrich. She said, "The doctor had." And she said something was like glass.'

Heimrich regarded her for a moment.

'That's interesting, isn't it?' he said. 'She didn't say which doctor, Miss Ross? Or what was like glass?'

She shook her head. The movement made her head ache; increased the pain along the side of her jaw, so that tendrils of pain reached down into her neck.

'And,' Heimrich said, 'you didn't see the person who hit you?'

'No,' she said. 'Whoever it was came up behind me when I was—'

'Show me,' Heimrich said. 'When you were what?'

'Like this,' she said, and moved out into the center of the hall and crouched. 'Near the foot of the stairs,' Lynn said. 'She was—Audrey was on her back, with one leg bent under her. I said something and started to reach out—to see if I could do something and—somebody grabbed me by the shoulders. Pulled me up.'

She stood up.

'And hit me,' she said. 'I don't know what with. Here.' She touched the right side of her

175

face.

'With a fist,' Heimrich said. 'At least, the doctor here says so. You didn't try to turn? To see who it was?'

'There wasn't time,' she said. 'And—and I was held so I couldn't move.'

Heimrich continued to look at her. But he spoke to Brian Perry. He said, 'Did you notice, doctor? The knuckles of the girl's right hand?'

'No,' Perry said.

'Bruised,' Heimrich said. 'Of course, she may have fallen on her hand when she was struck. That's probably what happened, naturally. She had quite small hands—was quite a small girl, really. You're quite sure Miss Ross was hit by somebody's fist, doctor?'

Perry moved closer to Lynn Ross, and then—although her head swirled, and fear swirled in her mind—Lynn stood very straight and tall (tall like a tree) and held her chin high. Perry did not touch her face, but only looked at it. He turned to Heimrich.

'You must know,' he said, 'that I can't be certain, captain. There's no sign of anything else. No break of the skin. Not a great deal of swelling.'

'No,' Heimrich said. 'There isn't, is there? Of course—' He did not finish. Sergeant Forniss came into the pantry through the door which led to the living room and Heimrich said, 'Yes, sergeant. Get through all right?' Forniss merely nodded. 'You'd better get the rest of them up, sergeant,' Heimrich said. 'They seem to be sound sleepers. You'd think the light would have wakened some of them—or the noise the truck made.'

'The truck?' Brian Perry said.

'Generator truck,' Heimrich told him. 'Oh, the power's still off, doctor. We're rolling our own.' He closed his eyes, momentarily. 'Not soon enough,' he said. 'However—you'd better go change, Miss Ross. Get some other clothes on. There's blood on your robe.'

'It happened the way I said,' Lynn told him, and spoke, by effort, in a level tone. 'I—I tried to lift her. That was how—'

'Now Miss Ross,' Heimrich said. 'I haven't said anything else, have I? Ray?' Heimrich raised his voice at that. Ray Crowley came through a door which led to the kitchen. 'The trooper'll go with you,' Heimrich said.

Lynn started to move. She swayed; felt herself swaying. Brian reached out a hand toward her, but she moved so that she was not touched. She said, 'I'm quite all right,' and turned and went toward the narrow stairway— went up it, using the handrails, and did not look round to see who followed her, but knew that Trooper Crowley came up the stairs behind her. She went along the narrow corridor, bright now, and down the intersecting, wider, hall to the door of her room.

'Minute, miss,' Crowley said and moved

177

around her and opened the door. He stepped into the room and switched on lights and looked around. 'All right, miss,' he said, and stepped back and let her go into the room. For a moment, inside, she hesitated. Crowley stepped farther back into the hall, and she closed the door and was alone in the bright, cold room. For a moment she merely stood there, and found she was shaking—that her whole body was shaking. And not only, she knew, because the room was cold, because light had not brought warmth with it. She listened, and did not, at first, know why she listened. Then she realized that she waited to hear the footsteps of the tall young trooper, walking away from the door on the bare boards of the hall floor. She did not hear him walk away.

She looked at her hands, and there was blood on her right hand. She shuddered, then, and suddenly, almost desperately, tore off the robe. There was blood on the robe, where the dying girl's head had rested. She threw the robe to the floor and then, still with a kind of desperation, she tore off what she had worn under the robe—pants, a slip—and threw them on the floor by the robe. There was a little blood on the slip.

She crossed the room to the bath, moving very fast, almost as if she fled. She tried first the faucet at the tub, but when she turned the knob marked 'Hot' only a trickle of water came, and that cold. For a moment, crouched at the tub, her hand in the trickle of freezing water, she felt complete defeat, and, again, the rise of sickness. But she stood, after a moment, and went to the wash basin. The water which should have been hot trickled there, too, and was cold; she turned the other faucet on, and the flow was better and the temperature no worse. She filled the basin and began to scrub her body with the cold water and a rough cloth—scrubbed first at the hand which had been in Audrey Latham's blood, and then at the shoulder against which she had held the girl's head.

But then, long after all the blood had been cleaned away, she went on scrubbing her body with the cold water on the rough cloth, until the skin began to redden and until—almost unbelievably—she felt warmth returning. She dried herself, finally, but still used a kind of violence, although one cannot rub away fear.

She dressed again in sweater and slacks, and warm socks and loafers over them, and as—almost unconscious of what she did—she sat at the dressing table and brushed her hair, she heard a metallic ping from the radiator. So in time there would be warmth. Then she heard someone knock, lightly at the door. She had been too long, she thought, and stood and was about to answer when someone outside, but quite near the door, said, 'Yes, sir?'

'Oh,' someone said—Brian Perry said, from

the other side of the door—'didn't see you, trooper.'

'No, sir,' Crowley said. 'I guess you didn't, doctor.' And then, after a moment, Crowley said, 'She's all right, sir. You were worried about her?'

'Just wanted—' Perry began, but by then Lynn had crossed the room and opened the door. The two men stood quite close together in the hallway. 'Apparently,' Brian Perry said, 'I needn't have been.'

Lynn did not look at either of them. She merely waited.

'He's getting everybody together downstairs,' Brian said. He reached out, apparently to touch her shoulder.

And she was afraid. Until she moved to avoid his hand, she had not realized how afraid she was.

'I didn't see who hit me,' she said, then, and spoke to a space between the two men. 'I didn't see at all.'

'Sure not,' Trooper Crowley said. 'Don't you worry, Miss Ross.'

Brian came so quickly, Lynn thought. *He was there as soon as the captain was!*

CHAPTER TEN

Brian Perry walked beside her down the hall toward the staircase. The oil stove still burned near the head of the stairs; still gave off the stench of burning oil. But the little circle of light it had thrown against the ceiling had been engulfed in greater light. At the end of the hall, under one of the front windows, a radiator made small, pinging sounds. They went down the stairs, and Trooper Ray Crowley walked close behind them. Lynn looked straight ahead; walked tall down the staircase.

Someone had removed the oil stove in the lower hall. (That was the thing to do. Think of the small things. Of the oil stoves; of the pinging sound from a radiator; or how bright the light was after darkness. Do not think that Audrey Latham's right hand was bruised, as if, trying to defend herself against death, she had struck out, futilely, with all she had. Do not think that Brian Perry had been in the pantry as soon as Captain Heimrich had, and that Brian had been fully dressed. *As if he had been waiting!* Think of the small, ordinary things.)

Outside, in the night, a motor was running. Listen to the running motor. A generator on a truck—think of the generator. For electricity, they were 'rolling their own.' Think of that. There are double doors from the hall into the living room; stand aside while Brian Perry opens the double doors. Go, walking tall, into a room in which there is, or will be, someone who brought a dull hatchet down—more than once; oh, evidently, more than once—on soft blond hair, on the fragile skull beneath the hair. Do not think of that—or of curved lips reddened carefully for the affairs of life—or of blood on them at the end of life.

The long living room was softly bright with the light of shaded lamps. From some place below there was a pulsation. It was like a heart beating. Think of that—that it is the heart of the house. But think of it prosaically—that is the oil burner, alive again. In time it will warm the house—this room, the halls outside—the storeroom where there is blood on worn linoleum. The pump will start—has started. In time there will be water in the house. A house lives by water as it does by heat. Think of the ordinary things.

It was warmer already in the living room, but that warmth came from the fire. Tom Kemper was sitting on his heels in front of the fire, prodding the fire with a poker, pushing kindling under the logs. The kindling was broken pieces from a case. One of the pieces had a stencil on it—it had been part of a case which had held champagne. (But do not think of that—of toasts to a New Year, of dancing in Brian Perry's arms, of the laughter of a bright-haired girl.)

Kemper turned and looked at them when they entered the room. He merely shook his head, commiserating all of them, and did not speak. He leaned down and blew on the fire, and the kindling came alight and small, bright flames began to lick around the dark logs. (One of the logs was charred; it would catch quickly. Think of the ordinary things.)

Tom Kemper wore a tweed jacket, with leather patches on the elbows, over a light sweater. He wore gray slacks.

Forniss was in the room, standing near a light. The door at the rear of the room opened and the Speeds came—small, plump people, at the distance and in the light oddly alike. They were fully dressed. Abner Speed wore a striped necktie.

'You wanted—' Abner Speed began, and Forniss did not wait for him to finish, but said, 'That's right. Sit down somewhere.' They sat, side by side, on straight chairs, at the end of the room.

Margaret Halley came in, after a few minutes. She wore a sweater and skirt; she was very trim, and looked much younger than she was—until one saw her face. Her face was white; her lips bloodless and unreddened. Her face was set, and had a curious, hard smoothness. It was as if the skin had been stretched tight over the delicate bones; as if it had shrunk against the bones. Margaret said nothing to the others in the room. She looked

183

at Forniss, without expression, and at the others not at all. She went to a chair and sat in it and looked at the reviving fire.

It was almost ten minutes later that Struthers Boyd came into the room—came slowly and heavily, wearing slacks and a coat sweater, which he had apparently put on over a pajama top. Boyd looked as if he had been dragged unwillingly from bed. He rubbed his eyes; he had the appearance of a man who has dressed in the dark and who has forgotten to brush his hair. Boyd pawed at his hair to flatten it.

'Can't believe it,' Boyd said, and his voice was as heavy as his body, as his movements. 'That pretty kid. Can't believe it.'

(The back of her head was crushed. When she was dying she bled from her mouth, Mr Boyd.)

Tom Kemper turned, at that. His mouth was working.

'Can if you try, Boyd,' he said, and his voice for the first time, was harsh. 'I think you can—'

(But you didn't see it, did you, Mr Kemper?)

'Take it easy,' Forniss said. 'Just everybody take it easy. Till the captain gets here.'

They turned to look at him.

'Plenty of time to talk,' Forniss said. 'After the captain gets here. All the time in the world.'

They continued to look at him, as if they expected him to go on, somehow to clarify. He looked from one to the other, and his eyes had no expression. (It was as if they had ceased to be people—people with names, with shapes which differed. It was as if, in Sergeant Forniss's eyes, they had become so many objects.)

Then that waiting—the wary, careful, observant waiting—began again. It was as it had been earlier. But now they moved less and Lynn, sitting tightly in a chair, thought that this was because no one wished to turn his back on the others—so to become defenseless; so to chance missing something, something inimical or revealing, which might go on while the back was turned. (And this time Audrey Latham did not, restlessly, prowl the room.) And this time Sergeant Forniss was not distant, by a window, seemingly indolent in his watching. Now he stood close, his face hard, his expressionless eyes moving from one to the other.

It seemed that they waited for a very long time. The small movements all of them made became increasingly abrupt; when there was the slightest sound, they turned their heads jerkily toward the sound—all except Margaret Halley, who was motionless. Actually, it was a little over half an hour by the watch on Lynn Ross's wrist. It had been twenty minutes of twelve (was it really so early?) when Forniss told them, in effect, not to talk to one another. It was a quarter after midnight when Captain Heimrich came into the room.

He carried the hatchet. He had looped a cord

185

around it, so that he did not touch the handle. The hatchet dangled from his hand. In the other hand, he carried a newspaper.

He walked to a table on which there was a lamp, and spread the newspaper on the table. Then he dangled the hatchet down and let it rest on the newspaper. He released the cord and, for a second, rubbed his hands together as if rubbing off something which clung to them.

'You two,' he said to the Speeds, in a voice at once weary and cold. 'You two come up nearer. I want everybody to see this.'

The Speeds got up, uneasily. They came closer to the fire. They stood and looked at the hatchet. 'Use it to split kindling,' Speed said, dully, staring at the hatchet.

The head of the hatchet was darkly stained—looked at, not touched, there seemed to be stickiness on the head of the hatchet. Involuntarily, Lynn's hand went up to the breast and shoulder against which she had held Audrey Latham, so that the ruined head rested there.

'Yes,' Heimrich said. 'There's blood on the hatchet. Blood—and brain tissue.'

Lucinda Speed, who had leaned forward, peered shortsightedly at the hatchet, gave a little cry. She backed away, a hand to her mouth. Heimrich watched her. His eyes were wide open enough now, Lynn thought. They were very blue. (I had a little pitcher once; a pitcher of blue glaze. That's the way his eyes are now. It must have been when I was a little girl I had the pitcher.) Lucinda Speed continued to back away. She shook her head; now she held both hands to her mouth. Heimrich looked away from her. He looked, in turn, at each of them.

'Well?' he said.

Struthers Boyd made a strange, gagging sound.

'She was—' he said, and stopped and began over. 'That's the way she was killed? The little blond girl.'

'There are a few hairs stuck in the blood,' Heimrich said. 'From the girl's head. Blond hair—yes, Mr Boyd. Yes, that's the way it was done. Somebody came up behind her, probably. At the foot of the back stairs. Struck her with the hatchet. Struck her several times. And yet—she lived a little while.'

(I could feel life in her; the tenseness of life; muscles tense with life. And then there was— nothing. Then there was only weight; That is the way people die. They grow heavy.)

'Miss Ross found her,' Heimrich said. 'Tell them, Miss Ross. What you told me. And— how you happened to be there. Happened to find her.'

(But I told you that. Didn't I tell you that?)

'Go on, Miss Ross,' Heimrich said. 'You and Miss Latham were sharing a room. You woke up and—what? Found her gone, I suppose?'

187

'I woke up,' Lynn said. 'She had been beside me. She—she was gone. She wasn't in the room and I looked in the bathroom and—I looked in the closet, too. Her things were gone.'

'Yes,' Heimrich said. 'She took her bag with her. And wore her coat. The bag was near the back door. She'd put it there, apparently, and then gone back. To meet whoever she'd arranged to meet. Go on, Miss Ross.'

'I don't know anything about that,' Lynn said. 'It happened the way I say. I just woke up and found she was gone.'

'And,' Heimrich said, 'went looking for her. And found her. How did you know—'

'Wait,' Lynn said. 'I told you about the light?'

Heimrich shook his head. He said, 'No, Miss Ross. You didn't get around to that.'

They all looked at her—looked at her and waited. She told about the light, but found it hard to tell. She said it was like the ghost of a light. And at that, Heimrich nodded slowly.

'If there had been someone at the foot of the stairs,' he said, 'someone using a flashlight to—to see whether he had done enough—it might have looked like that. Reflected up the stairs, along the hall, very faintly. Do you think it was that, Miss Ross?'

'I don't know,' she said. 'I—I suppose it must have been something like that. Wait—I thought that then. I remember now.' He looked at her. 'I *do* remember,' she said. And

188

then she said, quite steadily, 'Do you think I killed her? Why would I kill her?'

'Now Miss Ross,' Heimrich said. 'Why do you say that?'

'You said her hand was bruised. And—he' (she indicated Brian Perry with a movement of her head) 'he said someone had hit me with—with a fist. And—you sent the man to watch me. Unless—'

'Unless to protect you,' Heimrich said. 'But, go on, Miss Ross.'

'I found her,' Lynn said. 'I told you that. And then someone hit me and put us—put both of us—in the storeroom. I don't know why.'

'To gain time, probably,' Heimrich said. 'Go on. She talked a little—said words anyway.'

'I told you.'

'Again,' Heimrich said. 'So the rest can hear, Miss Ross.'

She repeated the words Audrey Latham had used. They all looked at her; listened to her.

'Before that,' Heimrich said. 'You were in the room with her. Did you talk then? You must have talked.'

'A little,' Lynn said. 'Nothing that seemed to matter except—she did say something about watching her step.'

'She didn't,' Heimrich said. 'Did she say anything about leaving the house? Trying to leave the house?'

'No.'

'But, earlier, she'd asked you to help her get away. Isn't that true?'

'I told her it wouldn't work. That it wasn't possible.'

'But she did ask you?'

'Yes.'

'And didn't bring it up again. When you were together in the room?'

'No.'

He waited for a moment. Lynn could only wait, too.

'That's all that happened, then?' Heimrich said. 'You talked for a few minutes. Then went to sleep?'

'I went to sleep,' Lynn said. 'I thought, from her breathing, she'd gone to sleep too. Now—now I suppose she hadn't. Was pretending to be asleep.'

'You didn't waken when she got out of the bed. Got her things together?' His tone was skeptical.

'No,' Lynn said. 'Wait. She must have done that before. I remember now. Must have taken her things into the room I'd been in. She brought my things in before I went up. She must have planned it then.'

'Yes,' Heimrich said. 'She'd made arrangements. Dr Perry?'

Brian Perry looked at Heimrich. The light flickered on his glasses, concealing his eyes.

'You hadn't gone to bed,' Heimrich said. 'When Miss Ross called out, you got there as quickly as I did. From the dining room? Or where, Dr Perry?'

'The dining room,' Perry said. 'That's right, captain.' Heimrich waited. 'I was sitting there,' Perry said. 'In front of the fire.'

'Waiting?'

'Until it was time to kill Miss Latham? No, captain. I was just sitting there.' He paused for a moment. 'Thinking,' he said.

'Remembering?'

Perry shrugged slightly. He said if Heimrich liked that better. He said that that had entered into it.

'Going back over things?' Heimrich said. 'Trying to remember if you had made a mistake? Whether you could—correct the mistake?'

'Not as you mean it,' Perry said. 'As I suppose you mean it. No.'

'Some one of you did,' Heimrich said. 'Thought Miss Latham's death would correct the mistake. Decided that she knew more than she had admitted knowing. Probably, had seen more.'

They all looked at him—all except Margaret Halley.

'Miss Latham went downstairs last night,' Heimrich said. 'After the rest of you had gone to bed. Or say you had. Went down to talk to Mr Halley. At least, she said that. And—'

'And saw me coming back upstairs,' Margaret Halley said. She did not look at

Heimrich, or at anyone. 'Coming back after I'd gone to see if John was all right.'

'And,' Heimrich said, 'coming back without having found out. And, she said, carrying something.'

They had, Margaret Halley said, still speaking to the fire, been over that. She had been carrying nothing.

'She imagined it,' Margaret said. 'But—not enough of it, did she, captain? Because, she couldn't remember what it was I was supposed to be carrying.'

'She said she couldn't,' Heimrich said. 'When I talked to her. She may have remembered later. It may have come back to her. Or—she may have lied to me, naturally. Have kept something back.'

He waited. Margaret Halley did not answer.

'It's dangerous to keep things back,' Heimrich said. 'Some of you still are, probably. I mean the ones who didn't kill, of course. Yes, Miss Ross?'

(How did I show it? How does he know?)

'Something that doesn't fit,' Heimrich said. 'Well, Miss Ross? You've remembered something? Something Miss Latham told you?'

They looked at her. For the first time, Margaret Halley turned from the fire, and looked as the others did—warily, measuringly.

'She said something about having been Mr Halley's protégée,' Lynn said. She spoke

192

slowly. She did not look at any of them, although she knew that they continued to look at her—to wait for her words. But it was not important; it was only a little thing. 'She said, "The way they mean it."' She stopped.

'She was lying,' Margaret Halley said. 'And—the captain knows that already.'

'That she was lying?' Heimrich said. 'You said before that she might have misunderstood. That you thought she had.'

'One thing or the other,' Margaret Halley said. 'It isn't important now. Not to you. Since both of them are—'

She did not finish.

Heimrich waited. Then he said, 'Go on, Miss Ross. It's true Miss Latham had told me that. And that Mrs Halley said she and her husband had talked the situation over. Were in agreement on it. But—go on.'

Lynn looked at him, then.

'You said, "Something that doesn't fit," she said. 'She told me that. But this afternoon she and Mr Kemper—in the hall upstairs—I'd gone to get my coat and started to come out of the room and—'

Tom Kemper laughed. It was a kind of snorting laugh. He said, 'Oh for God's sake.'

They turned to look at him.

'She saw me with my arms around the girl,' Kemper said. 'That's the big surprise, captain. The—the what? The incident of the straying protégée?'

193

Heimrich merely looked at him.

'She was jumpy,' Kemper said. 'That's all it amounted to. I came along the hall and startled her and she well, she suddenly got shaky. I said something like, "Take it easy, lady," and the next thing I knew she was holding on to me. So I held on to her, and patted her shoulder and said, "There, there," the way one does. And—'

But he had spoken more slowly, with less assurance, as he went on. And, when he stopped, he looked quickly at the others, and first at Margaret Halley. (Why, Lynn thought, he's looking around to see whether we believe him. But one does that when—)

'That's all there was to what Miss Ross saw,' Kemper said. 'When she opened her door and started out—and went back in again, full of tact and—'

Again he stopped. He had resumed with special resolution. It had seeped from his tone.

'Now Mr Kemper,' Heimrich said, 'I take it you saw Miss Ross? Since she said nothing about going back into her room.'

He hesitated. He went on with a kind of stubbornness.

'Well,', Kemper said. 'Yes—I got a glimpse of her. Didn't occur to me she'd think it important enough to pass on.' He did not look at Lynn. He began to rub the finger tips of his right hand with the tip of the thumb.

'I don't,' Margaret Halley said, to the fire, 'see the point of these trivialities, captain. If

194

Tom wants to—comfort a pretty young woman. Surely, captain.' She turned, then, and looked at Heimrich. 'Except, of course,' she said, 'it bears out what I told you. That there was nothing between Miss Latham and my husband.'

'Now,' Tom Kemper said, 'wait, Margaret. I said—'

'My dear man,' Margaret said. 'We heard you.' For the first time in hours her voice was not dead. It was light, almost casual. 'You made her jump. You—calmed her down.' She turned to Heimrich. 'How,' she asked, 'could anything be less important?'

Heimrich closed his eyes. He waited.

'What you ought to be trying to find out, captain,' Margaret Halley told him, 'is what Miss Latham saw that she didn't tell you. Not who—patted her on the shoulder. Who—' She looked at the hatchet.

'Now Mrs Halley,' Heimrich said. 'The one she threatened. We all know that. Or—the one who thought her a threat, naturally. It comes to the same thing. It was because of what she said, of course. About the stairs. What she saw on the stairs.'

Margaret Halley made a quick movement. She said, 'I keep telling you.'

'Yes,' Heimrich said. 'You do, Mrs Halley. But—that may not be what she meant. Or—not all she meant. One of you thought it wasn't, perhaps. You see—she was on a staircase

195

herself last night. The stairs to the cellar. She said, "What I saw on the stairs." She might have meant you, Mrs Halley. But—she might have meant what she saw *from* the stairs. When she was on the stairs. Looking for Mr Halley.'

He paused. He looked from one to the other.

'I don't get it,' Struthers Boyd said. 'I don't get what you're talking about.'

'Don't you?' Heimrich said. 'You, Mr Kemper? One of you does, of course. One of you was in the basement. She heard you. Thought it was Mr Halley and went part way down the stairs and called. And then turned on the light. One of you thought she saw too much. You, Mr Kemper?'

'In the basement?' Kemper said. 'What the hell's this about the basement? What's down there except—'

'Now Mr Kemper,' Heimrich said. 'The usual things. The furnace. A supply of wood—and kindling, of course. Old boxes to use as kindling. And—the light switches.'

He waited. Kemper shook his head.

'Dr Perry?' Heimrich said. 'You, Mrs Halley? Miss Ross?'

He waited a moment.

'Oh,' he said, 'one of you will tell me, in the end. It's in the character of one of you. To improve on things.'

'You give warning, captain,' Brian Perry said. 'Is it wise to give warning?'

(But it isn't that, Lynn thought. He ought to

know it isn't that. It's as if he—he were dangling something. Dangling it just out of reach. Watching to see who moves; tempting someone to move—to say the wrong thing. To do the wrong thing. He says, 'Something needs improving on.' He says, 'There's a flaw somewhere—a weak spot in your story somewhere. Repair the flaw. Strengthen the weak spot.' If I were the one I would be afraid. I would be afraid to speak. But I would be more afraid not to speak. Afraid to move. Afraid to stay quiet. Does he see me yet? Can I run yet? Or will he see me only if I run? Have I missed—)

'You mention the light switches,' Brian Perry said. 'Was there a—a trick about the switches?'

'Now doctor,' Heimrich said. 'Don't you know there was? Because—you spoke about the trick before, doctor.'

'About a trick,' Perry said. 'But—yes, I guessed there was a trick. Lynn and I guessed.'

(But *you* guessed. You told me. It wasn't I who guessed.)

'Yes, doctor,' Heimrich said. 'You guessed about a trick.'

He waited. Tom Kemper spoke quickly.

'Trick?' he said. 'What do you mean by trick?'

'Now Mr Kemper,' Heimrich said. 'You hadn't guessed? Worked it out. As Dr Perry did?'

197

'I don't,' Kemper said, 'know what the hell you're talking about.' He looked around at the others, his eyebrows raised in enquiry. 'What's he talking about?' he said.

'Beyond me,' Struthers Boyd said. 'Whole damn thing's beyond me.'

Margaret Halley did not respond. She looked into the fire. She sat, Lynn Ross thought, very tightly.

Kemper looked at Lynn. She started to speak.

'Tell them, doctor,' Heimrich said, to Brian Perry. 'Tell the ones who don't know.'

'What I guessed?' Perry said.

'Now doctor,' Heimrich said. 'What you guessed, of course.'

Perry told them. Heimrich nodded. He was, Lynn thought, now oddly like a teacher who approves a superior pupil. Or—*like a cat who has seen the movement of a hidden bird*?

'Yes,' Heimrich said. 'It was done that way. Mr Halley was tricked into going out. Followed. Killed.'

Again there was a pause. It seemed to Lynn that silence was very loud in the room.

'It is only theory,' Margaret Halley said. 'You could never prove it, could you?'

'Oh,' Heimrich said, 'it's proved itself now, hasn't it? The murder of Miss Latham proves it, naturally.'

She did not answer, except by a further stiffening of her body.

198

'When you went down to see if your husband had gone to bed,' he said. 'Decided that he had and went back up. As you say you did.'

'I did,' she said.

'Did you see anyone? Or—hear anyone?'

'No.'

'Did you go near the stairs to the basement?'

'I told you what I did. All I did. I stepped into the living room. Found it was empty. Decided John had gone up to bed and went up myself.' She paused, briefly. 'Carrying nothing,' she added.

'And,' Heimrich said, 'the rest of you were all in bed. You've all told me that.'

'That's right,' Kemper said. 'So?'

'Oh,' Heimrich said, 'one of you is lying, of course. One of you was in the cellar. Replacing the main switch.'

'Replacing?' Perry asked.

'Oh yes,' Heimrich said. 'Mr Halley was dead by then. Miss Latham turned the cellar light on. It went on. *Your* "trick" was finished, doctor.'

'Not my trick,' Perry said. 'You—use words loosely, captain.'

'Perhaps I do,' Heimrich said. 'The trick you described. One of you was in the cellar. Assumed Miss Latham had seen you. Decided to play another trick—offer to take Miss Latham away. To Katonah, at least. To the station, probably. And, instead—'

'Wait a minute,' Tom Kemper said. 'Wait

199

just a minute.' He leaned forward in his chair, leaned toward Struthers Boyd. 'Struth,' he said. 'You asked me about trains. Remember? Whether there was still a train to town? And, first, I said the last one was at ten something. Remember?'

'I thought—' Boyd said. (He's frightened. Should he move? Or is the danger in movement?) Boyd looked quickly at Heimrich, and then away again.

'And,' Kemper said, 'we looked it up to be sure, and found there was an extra train—an extra, late train on New Year's Day. A train at twelve twenty-something. You remember that, Struth?'

'Suppose I did?' Struthers Boyd said. 'Suppose I—' But then he stopped. He looked at Heimrich. Boyd's eyes were no longer sleepy. 'Deputy of yours, captain?' he said. 'Or, one of your stool pigeons?'

'Now Mr Boyd,' Heimrich said. 'I gather you were interested in the train times?'

'The girl wanted to get out of here,' Boyd said. 'You know that—she tried to get Miss Ross to drive her. She wanted me to. Said we could take the station wagon. She said there were chains on it.' He paused for a moment. 'I don't deny I thought about doing it,' he said. 'But I decided not to and told her I wouldn't, and she'd be a fool if she tried it. I said, it would look like we were running away, and I didn't have anything to run from and didn't think she

200

had. She said, "That's what you think."'

That, Boyd said, was all she had said. He had asked her what she meant, and she had merely shaken her head. Then, she had asked if there was still a train to New York.

'I didn't know,' Boyd said. 'She asked me to find out. Said if she asked, she'd give everything away, because already she'd tried Miss Ross and probably Miss Ross had—well, what she said was, "blabbed." She said—well, she said she wouldn't forget any help I gave her.'

'What did you—' Heimrich began. Then he said, 'Never mind. Go on, Mr Boyd.'

'That's all there was to it,' Boyd said. 'I asked Kemper. My old pal, Kemper.'

'Telling him it was Miss Latham who wanted to know?'

'Well,' Boyd said. 'No. I let him think whatever he wanted to. But—' His eyes narrowed slightly. 'But come to think of it,' he said, 'a couple of minutes later, I went out in the hall and Miss Latham came out after me, and I told her about the train. Kemper could have seen us, and put two and two together.'

'So,' Kemper said, 'could anyone. As a matter of fact, I didn't notice it. So if you're trying—'

'I'm not trying anything,' Boyd said. 'You brought it up.'

They both had raised their voices somewhat; both seemed angry. Lynn looked from the two men, leaning toward each other in their chairs, to Heimrich. He was not watching them. His eyes were closed. Boyd turned to him and, before Boyd spoke, Heimrich opened his eyes.

'All right,' Boyd said. 'That's all there was to it. I told her about the train, advised her to give the idea up and—well, I thought she had. That's all I know about it.'

'And,' Heimrich said, 'you knew—or anyway could guess—that Miss Latham would be going downstairs about the time she did go.'

'I told you,' Boyd said. 'I thought she'd given it up. I—'

'That,' Tom Kemper said, 'is what you say now, isn't it?'

And that brought Boyd to his feet; brought him threateningly to his feet.

'Sit down, Mr Boyd,' Heimrich said, and Sergeant Forniss moved toward Boyd. Boyd hesitated, sat down.

'Of course,' Heimrich said, 'Mr Kemper's right. It is what you say now, Mr Boyd. That you didn't plan—or tell *her* you planned—to drive her to the station. Didn't arrange to meet her in the garage. Didn't—'

'Didn't kill her,' Boyd said. 'That's what I say now, too. And—' But he did not continue. His big body seemed to slump in his chair.

Heimrich waited; they all waited. Struthers Boyd sat heavily in his chair, which was near the fire. He looked down at the floor. It was Margaret Halley who spoke next; spoke, after

202

the silence, rather abruptly, as if, having considered, she had finally made up her mind to speak. She said, 'Captain Heimrich,' and, as he turned to her, went on.

'It may mean nothing,' she said. 'But—in view of this—Mr Boyd had persuaded my husband to invest—to invest quite a good deal, I believe—in some project. John had come to the conclusion that the project was—' She hesitated, apparently choosing among words. 'Unsound,' she said. She hesitated again, and her eyes moved to Struthers Boyd. 'No,' she said. 'More than that. Fraudulent. He planned to give Mr Boyd a choice. To return the money or—if he did not, John was going to the district attorney.'

Then Boyd turned his heavy body in the chair and looked at Margaret Halley. Slowly, he shook his head. But there seemed, to Lynn Ross, to be a kind of numbness in his movement. Heimrich waited a moment. Then he said, 'Well, Mr Boyd?'

'What's the use?' Boyd said. 'She's lying. But—what's the use?'

'Lying?' Heimrich said. 'How, Mr Boyd? You deny the investment? Or—what do you deny?'

'He put up some money,' Boyd said. 'There was no secret about that. I—I told somebody about it. This morning, I think. Told—' He seemed to lose the thread momentarily. But then he looked at Brian Perry. 'Told you and

203

somebody,' he said.

'Yes,' Perry said. 'You talked about it. To me and Miss Ross. Some device you'd got hold of. A "thing," you said.'

'Going to revolutionize—' Boyd said. 'But there is a secret about that. When she says fraudulent, that's a lie.'

'It's what John said,' Mrs Halley told them. 'I don't say he went into detail. He was going to give Mr Boyd the choice, as I said.'

'And,' Heimrich said, 'invited him here for that purpose? It was your husband who invited Mr Boyd?'

'He suggested it,' Margaret Halley said. 'As for the actual invitation—I wrote the note, of course.'

'Yes,' Heimrich said. 'And—you wrote to Dr Perry, too?'

'What?' she said. 'What's that to do with it? Actually, I used the telephone. Didn't I, Brian?'

'Although,' Heimrich said, 'you had told him, earlier, I suppose, that your husband was responsible for the death of Dr Perry's wife?'

'You told him about that, Brian?' she said, and now leaned a little forward in her chair. Her hands twisted together in her lap. Brian Perry nodded, the firelight on his glasses.

'I—I stumbled into it,' she said, now to Heimrich. 'In trying to explain about John. But—why are you asking these things? When what Tom tells you—' She stopped.

And it was not clear, Lynn thought. Nothing was clear. A moment before, it had seemed that Struthers Boyd was at the center of a narrowing circle; that, slowly, carefully, he was being wrapped around in a net of words, of implications. But now—now?

A siren sounded outside—sounded once, in a lonely moan.

CHAPTER ELEVEN

Heimrich and Sergeant Forniss went out of the room together, but Trooper Ray Crowley, at a nod from Heimrich, remained. Heimrich took the hatchet with him, still dangling from the string. There was now no insistence that those in the room refrain from talking, but none of them seemed inclined to talk. Instead, they listened—listened to the sounds made by several men coming into the house, going down the hall. Now and then, from the rear, they could hear voices. Then they heard another car come up the drive. For a moment, the lights of the second car showed against the curtains, pierced into the room. Then the lights went out. More men came into the house and went down the hall.

Sergeant Forniss came back into the living room after a few minutes and they looked at him. 'Medical examiner,' Forniss said.

'Photographers. And the rest.' Then he stood and watched them. After another ten minutes or so, Heimrich came back, and sat down where he had been sitting. He said there were a few more points. He said, 'Mr Boyd,' and Boyd looked at him, dully.

'Last night,' he said. 'During the party—toward the end of the party—you were mixing drinks?'

'What?' Boyd said. 'Mixing drinks? I don't—'

'For Mr Halley, at least,' Heimrich said. 'He was drinking scotch, I understand? The rest of you kept on with champagne? After midnight, anyway?'

'My God!' Boyd said. 'Why would I remember that? Maybe I poured him a drink, if I happened to be at the bar. I don't remember one way or the other.'

'You did,' Tom Kemper said. 'I remember seeing you.'

'So I did,' Boyd said. 'So what?'

'Now Mr Boyd,' Heimrich said. 'Mrs Speed.'

Mrs Speed made a small gulping sound.

'This morning,' Heimrich said. 'When you were straightening up the room. You did do that?'

'What was wrong with that?' Lucinda Speed said. 'Far as I knew it was like any other—'

'Yes,' Heimrich said. 'There was nothing wrong with it, naturally. You found a full glass of rum punch? On a table?'

She nodded.

'Where?' Heimrich asked her, and she pointed to a table.

'Spoiled it was,' she said. 'Sitting there all night by the fire.'

'You emptied it out? Washed the glass and put the glass away?'

'What would you expect?'

'Oh,' Heimrich said, 'just that, naturally. Anybody would expect that. Mrs Halley?'

She said, 'Yes?' She said it quickly, as if she had had the word waiting.

'When you came down last night,' Heimrich said. 'To see whether your husband had gone to bed. Did you notice the glass of rum punch?'

'I told you that,' she said. 'You go over and over things. What are you looking for?'

'Now Mrs Halley,' Heimrich said. 'A picture. A method. A character that fits the crime. You left the rum punch there?'

'Of course,' she said. 'Mrs Speed told you that. She found it there in the morning. What can it possibly matter?'

'Now Mrs—' Heimrich began, and there was a knock at the closed double doors into the hall. Heimrich went to the doors, and out into the hall, closing them behind him. He came back after a few minutes and now, again, he was dangling the old hatchet—the hatchet with blood on its dull blade, a piece of twine looped around its rough, worn handle. He put the hatchet on the table and sat down again. He reached into his pocket and took out a small bottle, and put it on the table by the hatchet.

'Nembutal,' he said. 'The bottle you had somebody pick up yesterday, Mrs Halley. Or—picked up yourself?'

'How—' she said. 'Oh, it's dated, isn't it?'

'Yes,' Heimrich said. 'It's dated.'

'Mr Speed picked the capsules up,' she said. 'And—there was never any secret about it. I told you my husband had difficulty sleeping and—'

And then she stopped, suddenly, and looked at the little bottle. She got up, moving quickly, and walked to the table and reached out toward the bottle. She checked herself, and did not touch it, but bent to look at it.

'Yes,' Heimrich said, 'a good many of them used, Mrs Halley. Enough used to kill a man, wouldn't you say? If he wasn't treated quickly?'

She looked at him, said nothing for a moment. Then she said, 'But—surely you see now? Since the autopsy must have—'

He waited. She did not finish.

'I told you all earlier,' Heimrich said. 'Indirectly, I'll admit. Mr Halley was dying when he was killed—dying of barbiturate poisoning. Mrs Halley is right. The autopsy showed unabsorbed barbiturate in the stomach—a great deal of it. Quite enough to have caused death.' He paused. 'In time,' he said. 'Time that wasn't allowed.'

He turned, suddenly, to Brian Perry.

'You examined Mr Halley's body first, doctor,' he said 'You noticed nothing—nothing except the head injury, the indications of death by drowning?'

'No,' Perry said. 'I—lacked facilities for an autopsy, captain. Did you expect—'

'Now doctor,' Heimrich said. 'Did you look at the eyes?'

'Not particularly. You mean, for contracted pupils? But, they don't always contract. Sometimes they dilate instead.'

'Yes,' Heimrich said. 'And, if the barbiturate hadn't had time to work, there'd be nothing to show, naturally. How long would it take to work, doctor?'

Dr Perry assumed Heimrich meant from the time of ingestion? Heimrich nodded. Then various elements were involved—the kind of barbiturate taken, the quantity taken, the sensitivity of the taker. Nembutal, probably, Heimrich said; a very considerable quantity. As to sensitivity? He turned to Margaret Halley.

'Oh,' she said, 'no particular sensitivity. But don't you see—'

'In a moment,' Heimrich said. 'So, Dr Perry?'

'Twenty minutes,' Perry said. 'Or, up to an hour. There's no way I know of to be more exact. Of course, I'm not—'

'Captain Heimrich!' Margaret Halley said. *Listen!* It was as I told you. My husband wanted to die. He took an overdose. But before it took effect the lights went out and he—' She stopped. Heimrich looked at her and waited.

'No,' he said, when she did not go on, 'that leaves Miss Latham's death unexplained, doesn't it? It isn't that simple, is it? Where do you think your husband was when he—took the Nembutal, Dr Halley?'

'Why,' she said, 'I suppose—here. Where I left him.'

'But,' Heimrich said, 'the capsules were upstairs. He would have had to take them down with him, before the party started. Take them loose in his pocket? Why would he do that? Take some out of the bottle, leave the bottle there?'

She shook her head.

'I don't know,' she said. 'Perhaps he went up to his room and took the capsules. Perhaps he was there when the power failed. Perhaps— *what difference does it make?*'

Heimrich was shaking his head. She stopped speaking and looked at him.

'You were awake,' Heimrich said. 'Listening. Don't you remember? You went down because your husband hadn't come up.'

'I don't know,' she said. 'I might have dozed off. But—*what difference does it make*? He—he died of drowning.'

'Yes,' Heimrich said. 'He died of drowning.

And Miss Latham of being beaten. But—the Nembutal came first, didn't it? The start of the—yes, Mr Boyd?'

Struthers Boyd was no longer staring at the floor. Nor was he slumped in his chair. He had pulled himself up in the chair; was even leaning forward in it.

(Now they all run, Lynn thought. See how they run!)

'You're trying to make out I gave him this dope in a drink,' Boyd said. 'Is that it?'

'Now Mr Boyd,' Heimrich said. 'I haven't charged that.'

'And, don't,' Boyd said. 'Did you hear what the doctor said? Half an hour to an hour. Did you hear that?'

'Yes,' Heimrich said.

'If I mixed him a drink,' Boyd said, 'it was longer than that—a lot longer—before the lights went out and he went to start the generator. If that was the way it was. I went up early. Margaret was down a long time after that, according to what she says. Any stuff I put in anything would have hit him a lot earlier.'

'He might have let the drink stand,' Heimrich said. 'But—yes. I hadn't missed the point, Mr Boyd.'

'Well, then?' Boyd said. But Heimrich shook his head.

'Only the start of it, Mr Boyd,' Heimrich said. 'Perhaps not even that, properly speaking. It's conceivable Mrs Halley is right—that her husband planned to kill himself. Was, in a way, interrupted in the process.'

Boyd continued to lean forward.

'Captain,' he said, 'didn't you ever hear of fingerprints? If I'd taken the capsules out of this bottle—and apparently somebody did— wouldn't my prints be on the bottle and—'

And again Tom Kemper laughed. He shook his head. He said, 'For God's sake, Boyd, use your head!' And they all looked, then, at him.

'Of course he's thought of fingerprints,' Kemper said. 'Thought of them long ago. Don't play innocent, Boyd. No prints on the bottle, are there, captain? Because—a schoolboy would know enough to wipe them off. Just as there aren't any prints on the handle of the hatchet. For all his business about not touching it.'

If there was a gesture, Lynn Ross could not see it. But she saw Forniss, massive yet stepping with an odd lightness, move closer to the circle—closer to Boyd? To Tom Kemper? Or—to Brian Perry.

Heimrich did not move, did not change his position.

'Mr Kemper has a point,' he said, and spoke slowly. 'But—there are numerous prints on the bottle, Mr Kemper. Probably Mrs Halley's. Mr Halley's. Mrs Speed's. Probably, too the druggist's, and anybody else who handled the

212

bottle in the store. And—all badly scrambled, of course. Mrs Halley unwrapped the bottle, probably. Mrs Speed moved it in straightening up. Mr Halley moved it again, no doubt. Or— may have held it while he took out capsules, of course. And on the hatchet handle—*your prints are there, Mr Kemper.* Yours and Mr Speed's. But—*yours overlie his.*'

Slowly, his hands on the arms of the chair, Tom Kemper began to come out of it. His face was contorted.

'So *I'm* elected?' he said, and his voice rose as he talked. 'You have to frame somebody because you can't find things out—because you're no goddam good at your job—a lousy, crooked—'

Forniss reached out. He put a hand on either shoulder of Tom Kemper's, whose face was no longer the pleasant and open face of a man who lived by charm; whose face was ugly with violence.

'Now Mr Kemper,' Heimrich said. '*Why wouldn't your prints be there?* You'd used the hatchet to split kindling, hadn't you? Your prints could be there quite innocently.'

Forniss kept pressure on Kemper's shoulders. But now, it seemed to Lynn Ross, watching with wide eyes, that the pressure was not needed.

'*But you know they aren't*, don't you?' Heimrich said. 'Because you carefully wiped them off, didn't you? So, if I said they were still

213

there, you'd know I was lying. And—charge a frameup.'

He waited. Kemper merely stared at him.

'You couldn't let well enough alone,' Heimrich said. 'That was the trouble, wasn't it? From the start. I was to say the handle of the hatchet had been wiped clean. So you could say, "Well, that lets me out. Because my prints would be there innocently. I wouldn't *need* to wipe them off. But somebody else, who hadn't chopped kindling—Mr Boyd, say. Or Dr Perry—*he would have had to wipe his off.*" That was the idea, wasn't it?'

Heimrich reached out then and picked up the hatchet. No longer did he dangle it from the string. He took it by the handle, and turned it in his hands.

'A little learning—' he said. 'This is quite rough wood, Kemper. We wouldn't have got usable prints from it—nothing that would have harmed anybody. Only a thread or two from the cloth you used. And—*we didn't take your prints, Kemper*. For a man who's so handy around the house, you're not very handy at murder, Kemper. You do too many things you don't need to do.'

Kemper seemed, momentarily, to writhe against the commanding pressure of Sergeant Forniss's hands. '*You'll never*—' he said, in a voice high raised, shrill. But then he slumped again. 'I suppose she told you,' he said. 'It'd be all you'd have to go on.'

'Miss Latham?' Heimrich said. 'That she saw you in the basement? Is that what you mean?'

'*Tom*,' Margaret Halley said, and she was on her feet. '*Tom!* Can't you see what he's doing? What you're—'

'It's no good,' Kemper said. 'She had to see me. I didn't have time to get out of sight. It's no good, Marg. That's all he needed. It was clear enough what she meant about the stairs. About what she saw when she was on them. I thought maybe she hadn't told—' He broke off. 'Can't you see it's no good, Marg?' he said.

Margaret Halley sat again; she seemed to crumple into her chair. She put both hands over her face.

'You fool,' she said. 'You poor helpless fool. You—you've told him everything. Can't you see? *All he wants to know*.'

And then Heimrich said, in a flat voice, 'No, Mrs Halley. Not everything. Because—he didn't *know* everything, did he?'

Silence was deep in the room. The room, to Lynn Ross, seemed to darken with the silence.

'Not even,' Heimrich said, 'that he needed to kill no one. That Miss Latham hadn't seen him—hadn't seen anyone and—'

Kemper, still held in the chair by Forniss's heavy hands, made an odd, wordless sound.

'No,' Heimrich said. 'She didn't see you, Mr Kemper. She'd been walking around in the dark, you see. She turned the basement light on

215

and it was momentarily very bright. She said it was a bright light. But it isn't, it's quite dim. It was only bright enough to blind eyes which had got accustomed to the dark. She didn't see you, Mr Kemper. It wasn't you she threatened.'

He stopped. He closed his eyes. He said, 'Miss Ross,' and Lynn said, in a voice not like her own, 'Yes?'

'You can't remember any more about what Miss Latham said? When—just before she died. About the doctor—a doctor?'

'I told you—' Lynn said, and hesitated. '"The doctor had—" I think that's what she said.'

'Yes,' Heimrich said. 'She'd remembered. Enough to frighten her—not enough, she thought, to prove anything. Because, of course, she didn't know what it meant. Only—that she had remembered what she saw. That it must mean something, because it had been denied. So—she wanted to get away. Because she was afraid. Or, perhaps, because she planned some use, later, for what she remembered. Unless—*had she already approached you, Mrs Halley?*'

For a moment, Margaret Halley did not move. Then she sat erect in her chair, and again her face was expressionless. Nor did her voice have expression when she said, 'I don't know what you're talking about, Captain Heimrich.'

'No?' Heimrich said. 'Well, perhaps she hadn't. I can't be sure of that, naturally.

Perhaps she was merely—a frightened girl. Trying to run from danger. Not knowing what the danger was. Because—at worst it would have been only her word against yours, wouldn't it, Mrs Halley?'

'I don't,' Mrs Halley said again, 'know what you're talking about.' (But it's as if she's learned the words, Lynn thought.)

'Oh,' Heimrich said, 'the glass you were carrying up the stairs, doctor. The empty glass. The one that had had the rum punch in it. After you thought you'd killed your husband.'

Her almost black eyes showed no expression as she looked at Heimrich. And she did not say anything. She merely shook her head, and that just perceptibly.

But Tom Kemper began to laugh. His laughter was high pitched, shrill and wild in the room. From the sound of his laughing, he laughed at a hideous joke.

CHAPTER TWELVE

The Colonel sat with his back to the fire and looked thoughtfully at Captain M. L. Heimrich, New York State Police. It appeared that the Colonel's thoughts were sad, bordering on the melancholy. It seemed not unlikely, indeed, that the Colonel might at any moment break into tears. 'I don't know,'

Heimrich said, 'what you've got to cry about.' The Colonel appeared to consider this, but he made no reply. Nor did he cease to look fixedly at Captain Heimrich, who found himself somewhat at a loss for further words.

The room was extremely large. The fire, and the area around it, seemed an oasis of warmth and light in a vast dimness. Heimrich found his surroundings, not excluding the Colonel himself, entirely restful. He could not remember, indeed, when he had felt more pleasantly relaxed or—and this, actually, was an odd thing—more at home. A door at the far end of the big room opened, and Susan Faye stood in it a moment, looking back, saying something into the room she had left. She said, 'You do that, Michael,' and walked down the room to where Heimrich sat. Susan Faye was slender in slacks and a sweater. No, put it bluntly; Susan was thin. Her face was thin, but it was not as tired, as strained, as it had been when Heimrich had first seen it. Her widely spaced gray eyes were still grave eyes. She had high, square shoulders. Heimrich stood up as she came down the room and sat down again when she was seated.

'Michael has decided to think,' Susan Faye said. 'I told him to go to sleep and he said, "I've decided to think a while first." He didn't say what about.' She smiled at Heimrich. She had a wide mouth. 'He's a nice boy,' she said. 'Even if my own.' She looked at the Colonel, who now

218

was looking at her. 'He's not a very cheerful dog, is he?' she said.

'No,' Heimrich said. 'On the other hand, he's very large.' He was mildly surprised to hear himself say this, since it did not constitute a responsive answer. He was not sure that it constituted an answer of any kind. But there was really no need to be responsive.

'Perhaps that's it,' Susan said. 'To be so much larger than most probably puzzles him. You say she is very tall?'

'She?' Heimrich said. 'Oh—Miss Ross? Not in the sense that the Colonel is a very large dog. A little above medium height. Five ten, perhaps. Why, Mrs Faye?' She looked at him. 'Susan,' he said, comfortably.

'And attractive?'

'I suppose so. I didn't think about it, particularly. It didn't seem to enter in.'

She nodded, her eyes unchanging in their gravity. But the corners of her wide mouth twitched for an instant. Heimrich, who is an observant man, observed this. He did not see that he had said anything to amuse her, but was pleased that he had. He was pleased with everything—he had been pleased since, telephoning Susan Faye earlier in the day, he had been invited to come to dinner. (If he didn't mind what was in the house.) He had been increasingly pleased with everything as, driving between large boulders (the driveway *did* constitute a hazard, there was no blinking that) he had skidded slightly on the insufficiently plowed, too steeply mounting, road up to the house which had been a barn. He had been most pleased to see Susan Faye standing in an open door, with the light behind her; with young Michael, who now was going on eight, beside her; with the Colonel, who was large even for a Great Dane, peering between them and, it was evident even from a distance, peering morosely.

Heimrich had felt, unexpectedly, like a man coming home after a long day at the office. It had been, later, quite natural that he should tell Susan Faye about his day at the office—although the 'office' had been a large, wind-swept house some thirty miles away, and the 'day' now some three days past. She had, of course, asked to be told—that was after Michael had retired to his room to do some reading. ('I've decided to read a while, now.') She had heard most of it when it had been time to tell Michael it was time to go to bed.

'Actually,' she said now, 'it was all a mistake, in a way, wasn't it? Mr Kemper's mistake?'

It could be called that, Heimrich agreed. Not, naturally, that murder wasn't always.

'And neither knew what the other planned,' Susan said. 'And either plan might have worked without the other. Except that the electric blanket went off.'

Mrs Halley's plan to kill her husband might very easily have worked, Heimrich agreed. In a sense, it had worked.

'As long as she doesn't talk,' he said, 'it's very unlikely we can get an indictment. It's unlikely we'll even try, although she's guilty of attempted murder.'

'You know and can't prove,' Susan said. 'Does that often happen?'

It happened rather often, Heimrich admitted. It would happen oftener if murderers were not so often talkative. Dr Margaret Halley did not appear to be the talkative type. Thomas Kemper, on the other hand, talked rather freely, once he was got started. But, he could say nothing to help them against Mrs Halley, because about that he knew nothing—and had known nothing at any time.

'See if I have it straight,' Susan said. 'She decided to kill her husband. She tells everyone that he is in a depression and may attempt suicide. She invites people all of whom have—or might be thought to have—some motive for killing him. Except Miss Ross? Why Miss Ross?'

'Record of depression,' Heimrich said. 'Unstable personality. Although she doesn't seem to have, actually. Another red herring.'

'Faint red,' Susan said. 'And these—in case suicide wasn't believed in? She was thorough.'

'Very,' Heimrich agreed. 'Second line of defense. Although, she shouldn't have needed it.'

'And,' Susan said, 'puts Nembutal in the rum punch. Expecting him to drink it, go upstairs and to bed, to die in bed.'

'Yes,' Heimrich said. 'Otherwise, she'd have taken the bottle of capsules downstairs, naturally. As a matter of fact, she assumed he had gone up to bed. When she didn't find him downstairs. Assumed everything had worked as planned. He'd drunk the rum punch. Therefore, he was dying.'

'It's complicated about the rum punch,' Susan said. 'Or, I'm stupid.'

'She poured two glasses of rum punch,' Heimrich said. 'Put Nembutal in one and gave it to him. Took the other upstairs herself, telling him she was going to drink it. Went down, when she thought she had allowed time enough, took the glass he had emptied, substituted the glass she had not touched. Took the empty glass back upstairs and washed it. That's what the Latham girl was trying to tell Miss Ross. Not that something was like glass. That what Mrs Halley was carrying was a glass.

'So, one of two things happens. What actually did happen—Mrs Speed finds a glassful of rum punch and pours it out and washes the glass. And so can prove that Halley didn't drink the rum punch. Or, somebody else finds it—Mrs Halley herself, perhaps. If she does, she makes a point of it. So proving the stuff wasn't in the rum punch. Or, if circumstances indicate, pours the rum punch out but leaves enough for analysis. Again, proving Nembutal wasn't in the rum punch.'

They watched the fire. The Colonel stood up. He walked behind Heimrich's chair and lay down between Heimrich and Susan Faye. The Colonel put his large muzzle on his enormous forepaws and gazed sorrowfully into the fire.

'How did you know it was Kemper?' Susan said, to the fire.

'Character,' Heimrich said. 'The murder was opportunistic. It needed a storm. If the power had failed on a calm night, Halley would merely have assumed a minor breakdown somewhere. Wouldn't have bothered to go down and start the generator. Mr Kemper has lived by being an opportunist. Also—he'd been very busy around the house. He was the one who got the wood. And so would have known about the hatchet. Also, although he was always looking for ways to be helpful, he didn't offer to go down to start the generator later. Boyd did that. Kemper knew it wouldn't do any good. He knew where the rotor was. In the lake. Also—'

'In other words,' Susan Faye said, 'you guessed.'

Heimrich considered that. He thought of amplifying—of explaining that one finds character to fit the crime. He said, 'Perhaps it comes to that, Susan.' He observed that, again, the corners of her mouth twitched slightly. He had never, he decided, felt more at home anywhere.

In fact, Heimrich thought then, he was probably making himself too much at home. He said that, perhaps, he had better be going, although without, immediately, making any move to go. She turned to him then, and looked at him very gravely.

'It's quite early,' Susan Faye said. 'It's not late at all, my dear.'

The Colonel snored, heavily. But neither of them really heard him.

* * *

Cannel coal burned softly in its basket under a marble mantel. Brian Perry had taken his glasses off. She would never, Lynn Ross thought, understand when he had reason to take them off and when to leave them on. Some people put glasses on when they planned to read, and others when they planned to drive. With Brian there did not seem to be any such established order. He's very different when he isn't wearing glasses, Lynn thought. He—

'Are you going to sleep?' Brian Perry asked.

'Relaxing,' she said. 'There's a lot to relax from, even after—how long is it? Four days?'

Her apartment was high above the street—so high that the night noises of the street were distant; were no more than components of the surge of sound which is a part of New York—so much a part that it is accepted, barely heard. Across the street, Central Park's lights were white on snow, and that was all the snow that was left in the city— all that mattered of the snow. In the apartment, one heard no wind. When one touched a light switch, light was inevitable, not a thing to be hoped for.

'You know about such things,' Lynn said. 'So—why, Brian? Only for the money?'

She flattered him, Brian Perry told her. But, so far as Kemper was concerned, it probably came to that. He was getting older; getting close to the time when he would no longer be in demand as a charming guest—as the gay young man first thought of when an extra man was needed, paying for the loan of luxury with the interest of ready availability and handiness about the place.

'A man,' Brian Perry said, 'has to look ahead. To, say, marrying a woman with a lot of money. But, Margaret didn't have it. Her husband had it. As simple as that.'

'But,' Lynn said, 'they didn't show it. That they were—' She paused. 'In love seems an odd way to put it,' she said.

'Very,' Brian told her, but then he, too, hesitated. 'As far as she was concerned,' he said, 'perhaps not so odd. As for showing it—it would be rather to the point that they didn't. Hence, in case anyone might be getting the right impression, his pass at Miss Latham. The

225

carefully stumbling, not to be believed, explanation. Misdirection.'

'Wait,' Lynn said. 'Audrey Latham knew about them. It must have been that. I—I was passing her room and heard her talking to Dr Halley. And she said—"Don't think I don't know about you and—" And then I went on. It didn't mean anything, then.'

'Halley undoubtedly knew,' Brian said. 'Probably told his—protégée. Her admission that she knew—the fact she had told Margaret she knew—probably was one of the things that frightened her—made her try to run.' He paused for a longer time. 'Margaret was in love with Kemper,' he said.

'How can you know?' Lynn asked.

He smiled suddenly, rather widely. He said, 'Thanks, my dear. Of course, I don't *know*. Any more, I suppose, than our good captain *knew*. He guessed. I guess. But—that's part of any diagnosis, my dear. Part of his diagnosis, too, I suppose. It isn't as simple as adding a column of figures; knowing there's a right answer, if you add right. If it were, among doctors, one diagnosis would be as good as another, one diagnostician as able as the next. We listen. We prod. We take pictures. We do basics, and make counts, and run chemical tests. And—it still isn't always a column of figures, with one answer—one answer that's inevitable. Sometimes you put together what you can find out and you say, "Well, it looks like—'' And then, you go on what it looks like. Some of us are better at it than others. I suppose some policemen are better than others are. I think Margaret was in love with Kemper. I don't suppose she had many illusions about him. She knew that if he was going to marry anyone—and particularly a woman a good bit older than he was—well, he'd want the woman wealthy. So—she tried to arrange it.'

He looked at her, watched her face.

'Don't let it get you down,' he said.

She shook her head. She said it was that Margaret Halley had always seemed so—'so serene. Able to look at things so clearly.'

He shook his head, then.

'The patient must feel that,' he said. 'That there is—certainty. As you say, serenity. Otherwise, it's no go, of course. But—under that, we're like the rest of us, my dear. All—higgeldy-piggeldy and every which way.'

He took a cigarette. He said, 'Damn,' and offered a cigarette to Lynn. But then he lighted his cigarette and threw the match into the fireplace. He looked at her unlighted cigarette and said, 'I'm hopeless.' He lighted it.

'Nothing will happen to her?' Lynn said. 'I mean—prison?'

'I don't know,' Brian said, and drew on his cigarette, and looked at her. 'She will get older. Very rapidly, now, she will get older. By herself.'

He drew deeply on his cigarette. Then he

snapped it into the fireplace. He leaned toward her.